The Raiders

A raid on a money shipment in the town of Appsley leaves a sheriff and a guard dead and another man wounded.

Lawman Pete Hewitt is sent to keep order until the town council elects another sheriff. A chance discovery convinces Hewitt that someone in town could also be involved in the raid and a storekeeper's murder confirms his suspicions though most believe the events to be unrelated.

Problems escalate when Hewitt antagonizes a gunman called The Count and when it looks as if he can unmask the villains his life is in great danger. Can he survive long enough to run the law-breakers to ground?

The Raiders

GREG MITCHELL

A Black Horse Western

ROBERT HALE · LONDON

Typeset by
Derek Doyle & Associates, Shaw Heath
Printed and bound in Great Britain by
CPI Antony Rowe, Chippenham and Eastbourne

ONE

George Mawson glanced at his watch and took his shotgun from the rack above his bunk. The breech was open and the brass ends of two cartridges showed in the twin barrels. He snapped the weapon closed and cradled it the crook of his elbow. It was time to start earning his money. A tall, angular man in his mid-forties, his face was heavily lined and tanned like old leather. But riding shotgun, exposed to the elements on the box of a stagecoach did that to people. He would be guarding a strongbox today on the ninety-mile run from Appsley to the bank at Carter Springs. It had been held overnight in the Appsley branch of the bank. He did not know how much money was involved but knew it was enough to tempt some of the bandits who periodically plagued the coach road.

Mawson had always considered himself lucky that the coaches he guarded had never been robbed, but many who knew him attributed that to the reputation he had earned with a gun during his early career as a law officer. He was a man, too, who made his own luck by careful preparation and today was no exception. He knew that the Colt .44 on his right hip was fully loaded and that both barrels of his twelve-gauge gun were charged with heavy buckshot.

Jamming his battered brown hat on his already greying hair, he walked out through the coach line office to where the Concord coach, with six impatient matched bays, was waiting. Alf Greer was already on the box seat handling the reins as a couple of stablemen held the heads of the leaders. He could see that the few passengers had taken their places. It was still early in the morning and no early risers had yet showed themselves on the streets of the little cattle town. Though it was a scene he had experienced many times, Mawson remained alert.

'Box's coming,' the driver announced.

The guard stepped around the back of the coach to see a worried bank employee walking towards them carrying a small but heavy box and Ross Anderson, the town sheriff, walking beside him with a Winchester carbine cradled in his arms.

'Howdy George,' the sheriff greeted. 'You have a good day for a ride. Let's hope that the road agents stay away so you can enjoy it.'

Mawson was about to reply, then momentarily froze with shock. A horseman with a bandanna over his face came spurring out of a nearby alley with a gun in his hand. The realization of what was

6

unfolding shocked the guard back into action. Even as he shouted a warning to his companions and threw the shotgun to his shoulder he saw other riders following. Working now on instinct he cocked both hammers and swung the twin muzzles of his gun towards the leading rider.

'Let 'em have it, Ross!' he called to the sheriff and loosed both barrels at his target.

The shotgun seemed to explode. A sheet of red flame flashed from one side of the gun, pieces of metal smashed into his face and with ringing ears, he dropped the weapon and staggered, half-blinded and shocked, his face a mask of blood. His right hand did not seem to be working properly and his movements as he reached for his revolver were slow and strangely clumsy. The nearest rider fired two close-range shots into him and the guard's world went dark. It is doubtful that he heard the shots that cut down the sheriff.

In seconds all was confusion, horses galloping about kicking up dust, guns firing, noise, death and chaos taking control.

The unarmed stable hands let the leaders go as they fled seeking cover. Freed of restraint and panicked by the shooting, the coach team bolted, dragging screaming passengers and trailing a plume of dust behind them. The severely wounded bank employee was in no position to resist when a rider leaned down, snatched the handle of the strongbox, pulled it to the saddle in front of him and galloped out of town.

In less than a minute the main street of Appsley had been transformed into something resembling a battlefield. A haze of powder smoke mixed with the dust kicked up by the coach hung in the air and three men lay bleeding into the dirt on the street.

Deputy Sheriff Pete Hewitt studied the buildings as he rode down Appsley's main street. His blaze-faced sorrel, recently purchased from a cattle ranch, did not like towns and snorted nervously as it saw people coming and going from doors, glinting window glass and odd pieces of paper being blown about in the light wind. 'Get used to this, Cactus,' he said to the horse. 'You're working for the law now.' Mulligan, his brown packmule strolled along behind. He was more familiar with towns.

Few people took much notice of Hewitt because horsemen in the streets were a daily occurrence and there was little about the young man to attract attention. He was of average height and build, with dark-brown hair, and was dressed like a cowhand although his clothes were a bit cleaner and his brown boots had been recently polished. Only those who looked closely would have noticed that the Colt .44 on his right hip had received more attention than range men usually gave their guns.

Hewitt soon found the place he sought. It was the office of John Grey, the town's only lawyer and elected mayor. He dismounted, hitched his animals to the rail and entered the building. A middle-aged woman wearing glasses looked up from her desk as he entered. 'Can I help you?'

'Yes, ma'am. I'm Pete Hewitt from the county sheriff's office. I was sent over here to help out until you people can get yourselves a new sheriff. I was told to see Mr Grey.'

'He won't be long, Mr Hewitt. Would you care to take a seat?'

'If it's all the same to you, ma'am, I'll wait here by the door where I can keep an eye on my horse. He's not used to towns and I don't want him to break my bridle or pull your hitching rack down.'

'Horses,' the lady said and frowned. 'Sometimes I think they are more trouble than they're worth.' Then she smiled and extended a hand. 'I'm Veronica Cook. We will probably see a lot of each other while you are here. I look after some of Mr Grey's office work. He has a client with him at present. You keep an eye on that mad beast and I'll call you as soon as Mr Grey is free.'

Cactus relaxed a little when he saw his master standing in the doorway but Hewitt saw a couple of ladies in dresses approaching with parasols. The horse had not seen any of these and would be sure to take fright. He quickly unhitched his reins and held them as the ladies went by. Cactus snorted and raised his head but was not too alarmed. His owner patted his neck. 'You're going well, Cactus. There's nothing wrong with being a bit wary of women but they rarely eat horses. Most of them are tame.'

'I'm glad to hear that,' said a soft female voice behind him.

He turned to see a pretty girl who had just left the lawyer's office. Laughter sparkled in her bright blue eyes and a smile was on her lips. Her neat yellow dress set her figure off superbly and her glossy brown hair showed beneath a stylish bonnet. Against the drabness of the town the girl stood out like some exotic decoration.

'John Grey asked me to tell you that he can see you now,' the girl said with a smile. 'You really shouldn't be frightening that poor horse about women.' She reached out gently and stroked the animal's white blaze. 'That wasn't so bad, was it?' Cactus seemed to agree and relaxed completely.

The same could not be said for his owner. Hewitt was flustered, trying to tip his hat and fasten his reins again at the same time. 'Thanks,' he managed to stammer as the vision seemed to glide away along the boardwalk.

Grey was a large man of about fifty and his expensive brown suit would not have looked out of place in a more affluent city. The gold watch chain across his middle seemed as if it was a safety measure to restrain a stomach that threatened to break out of his waistcoat.

His manner was smooth and courteous, if anything a little too smooth for the deputy's liking. He was more accustomed to less-refined characters who spoke their minds.

'It was a terrible business,' the lawyer said gravely as he explained the situation. 'We lost as good a sheriff as any town could have, the stageline lost a very good man and young Tom Ford from the bank was wounded – a really bad business all round.'

'Any idea who did it?'

Grey shook his head. 'There's no shortage of bad men in the hills around here. Those raiders could have been any of them.'

'How did they know about the money shipments?'

'It was no great secret. Any observant person who lived here for a while would soon learn that these shipments occur regularly. Bank employees and stage company people all knew and I suppose it was inevitable that word would soon reach the wrong ears.'

'I'll ask around while I'm here and see what I can find out. If that gang hit the town once, they can do it again. Next time it could be the bank.'

Grey sat back in his chair and fiddled absently with a paper knife. 'I'm not sure there's a lot one man can do, but we expect you to try. Your main job here, though, is to keep the peace until we can get ourselves a new sheriff. We have a nice orderly town here and we want to attract more business, but people won't invest in some hell-raising cow town.'

Grey told Hewitt that he could stay at the sheriff's office and have his meals at the hotel. The town would pay for those. There was a corral with stables

11

and a supply of fodder for his animals behind the office. A man would come in once a week to clean the premises. He was welcome to use any weapons or ammunition left in the office should the need arise. There were no set working hours as long as he stayed alert and stopped trouble before it got started.

'I'd better get settled in then,' the deputy said as he rose to his feet. Then as an afterthought he asked, 'Who was that lady who was here before me?'

Grey chuckled. 'Why did I think you would ask this question? That's Sue Macgregor. Her family owns the general store. She's some looker and a nice person with it. Half the single men in town want to marry her. You're welcome to join the queue.'

Hewitt put on his hat. 'I think I'll have to leave her to the others.'

The lawyer pushed back his chair and produced a bunch of keys from a desk drawer. 'Here are the keys to the sheriff's office. It's about a hundred yards down the road on the left. Welcome to Appsley.'

TWO

Hewitt did not take long to settle in, and as soon as he had cared for his animals he made a beeline for the stage company office. To his surprise he recognized the manager.

John Wilcox was the same worried-looking man who had worked in the railroad booking office at Hadleys Bridge where Pete had first worked as a deputy. He was only a couple of years older than Hewitt but was taller, thinner and more stooped, looking ten years older than his thirty years.

'So you're working for a slower means of transport these days,' the deputy said with a smile.

Wilcox smiled and extended a hand. 'Pete Hewitt. I didn't expect to see you over here. Have you come to solve our crime problem?'

The deputy shook his head. 'I think it will take a smarter man than me but I will find out as much as I can about the killings here while the witnesses still remember. Have you got time to come outside and show me where it all happened?'

'Sure, but I can only show you where people were killed. I was inside when the raid started.'

They went outside and Wilcox showed where the shot men had fallen. He also pointed out the alley from which the riders had emerged. He added that the coach driver, an important eyewitness, was out of town and would be returning the following day.

As Hewitt stepped from the boardwalk he noticed something metal on the ground. Bending to retrieve it, he saw something else shining just under the edge of the boardwalk. He picked up both pieces; a blackened, jagged piece of metal and a distorted circular piece of brass.

Wilcox glanced at them. 'Looks like bits of George Mawson's shotgun. It blew up in his face. It was a company gun with Damascus barrels. Sounds like the whole shebang just gave way.'

Hewitt nodded. He was aware that Damascus steel barrels, once fashionable, were now known to have too many flaws in their construction and could not withstand high pressures. 'Was Mawson loading his own cartridges?'

'No. The company supplied them. I still have the box and a few cartridges in my office. They are just the usual factory-loaded ones.'

The piece of steel was certainly from a Damascus barrel and bore a pattern left by the forming process. The brass disc turned out to be the base of a shotgun cartridge and a piece of shredded green cardboard was all that remained of the shell that normally would have been attached. Hewitt glanced at it. 'This doesn't look like the usual twelve-gauge cartridge base.'

'He might have been supplying some of his own cartridges but that bit of brass could have already been there and have nothing to do with the killings.'

'I don't think so. It would be more tarnished if that was the case. What happened to the rest of Mawson's gun?'

Wilcox shrugged his shoulders. 'I don't know for sure. I remember seeing it. It was a total wreck. But if you don't mind me saying so, that old gun won't help you find out who committed this crime.'

'I guess you're right,' the deputy said as he transferred the two pieces of metal to his vest pocket. 'Is that wounded bank clerk well enough to have visitors?'

'Probably. He's recuperating at home. He lives in the street behind this one. I'll tell you how to find the house.'

'Just one more thing. With such an important money shipment, why wasn't the bank manager with the strongbox?'

'I don't know,' Wilcox admitted. 'You'll have to ask him that yourself. Dave Basset's not the sweetest character in town but he might be a bit more civil to you than he is to the rest of us.'

Hewitt followed Wilcox's directions to the house of Tom Ford, the young bank clerk who had been wounded in the robbery. He found him propped up in bed with a very anxious mother hovering about him. His left shoulder was covered in bandages and he still looked pale and a little shocked. The deputy introduced himself and apologized for disturbing him.

'I don't think I'll be much help to you,' the clerk said. 'It all happened so quickly. Horses came tearing out of the alley, shooting started and George's gun seemed to explode. I saw the sheriff go down and tried to run for cover but a bullet hit me from behind and sent me flying.'

Hewitt frowned. 'Men shooting from galloping horses with six-guns usually don't shoot that well. Are you sure that they shot you?'

'Who else could it have been? I was a bit puzzled though. The doctor said that the bullet went in the back of my shoulder and came out the front. The last thing I remember was seeing a rider coming at me but I could have turned away to run. That's what I was intending to do when I found that the gun was caught in my pocket. It was all over in seconds.'

'Did you see anything unusual about the raiders?'

'Not really. There was no time to see details.'

'Where was your boss while all this was happening? I thought he would have been overseeing such an important cash shipment.'

'Mr Basset is retiring soon and he is gradually pushing more work on to me in case I have to look after things before a new manager is appointed.'

'Thanks for the help. I'll pay a call on Basset now. If you think of anything unusual or just remember something else that might be important, will you let me know?'

'I sure will,' Ford assured him.

Hewitt's next stop was the bank. A clerk ushered him into an office where a thin, middle-aged man was seated at a desk with a pile of papers on one side and a couple of ledgers on the other. There was no greeting in the narrow, hatchet face with its pale-blue eyes. When the deputy introduced himself the banker's handshake was limp and formal.

'I would have thought,' Basset began, 'that you would be out after those killers. You won't find them here in town.'

'Who knows where I'll find them? There's no point in chasing around the countryside until I know what to look for. It helps to know who you are chasing. I am interviewing witnesses and it would be helpful if I could hear your version of what you saw that day.'

'I didn't see much. I was inside the bank when I heard an explosion and shooting. I looked through the window and saw three riders charging at the coach. Mawson was down. I saw the sheriff spin around and fall. Young Ford dropped the strongbox, he seemed to be reaching for the bank pistol he had in his pocket. A bandit rode at him firing and suddenly he was on the ground. Around that time the coach team bolted. I saw one of the raiders

17

snatch the strongbox off the ground and the three of them galloped out of town.'

'How much money was in the box?'

'Eight thousand dollars.'

'Tell me about the man who picked up the box. What sort of mask did he have? Was he big or small? Anything about his horse?'

'I think he had a blue bandanna around his face. His horse was just an ordinary-looking bay or brown animal. I just remembered though – he was tall. He must have had long arms to be able to reach down and grab the handle of that box. It would take a strong man too, to lift that box one-handed and pull himself upright in the saddle again.'

Basset was growing impatient with the questioning. 'That's all I can tell you, Deputy. Now I have work to do. You should be after those three men, not worrying me.'

Hewitt rose to leave. 'Did it ever occur to you that more than three men could have been involved? I am beginning to think that those killers might have had a bit of help from someone here in town.'

Basset's face contorted in an expression of rage. 'Are you accusing me of being in cahoots with those raiders – of robbing my own bank?'

As he walked out through the door the deputy said over his shoulder, 'At this stage I am making no accusations against anyone. But nobody, and that includes you, Mr Basset, has been ruled out of complicity in this crime. This was not some opportunistic attack by out-of-work cowhands. I think someone who knew how things worked did a lot of careful planning.'

Basset's face turned red with rage. 'You can think what you like but you can't insult me and expect co-operation,' he shouted.

But Hewitt had reached the same conclusion, and by the time the banker had finished his outburst he was already gone.

THREE

Later Hewitt returned to the stage office. He had intended having another talk with Wilcox but from the boardwalk he could see the company man through an open window at the side of the office. He was talking to a person who looked like a farmer in his Sunday-best clothes, obviously another customer for the next day's coach. Rather than interrupt, he returned to the sheriff's office and jotted down some of the information he had gathered while it was still fresh in his mind. Idly he took the brass cartridge base from his pocket and examined it. As he rubbed at a blackened section of the brass numbers started to appear. With a bit more cleaning, he could discern the figure 20.

Then it dawned on him. The brass was not from the guard's twelve-gauge but from a slightly smaller twenty-gauge. Had it not been with a piece of the Damascus barrel, he would have seen the discovery as being irrelevant but suddenly a new aspect of the case had emerged.

Hewitt tossed the pieces in a desk drawer, left the office and went back to see if Wilcox was free. He found the company man preparing to close the office for the night.

'Did you learn much today, Pete?'

'Not really,' the deputy replied. 'It all seemed to have happened so quickly that none of the witnesses could recall much later.'

Wilcox laughed. 'I suppose Basset didn't tell you much. He's not noted for being helpful. He would not give you a fright if he was a ghost. I know that I shouldn't be carrying tales, but some folks here suspect that it could have been an inside job with Basset himself taking a cut.'

Hewitt refrained from expressing an opinion. Instead he asked, 'Do you still have some of those cartridges from the box that Mawson had in his gun?'

'Sure have.' Wilcox indicated a door behind him. 'That's the messengers' room where guards can rest overnight if they don't live in the town.' He opened the door to reveal a bunk, a table and chair, and a wall rack for a gun. 'If you look in that box on the table, you'll find a few cartridges still in it.'

Hewitt opened the box, took out one of the red buckshot cartridges, examined it for a while and replaced it. He pointed to the empty gun rack. 'I suppose that's where the guard's gun was kept?'

'That's right.'

'Was the gun kept loaded?'

'No – too dangerous. But George would compromise. He would load the gun when he came on duty and leave the barrels broken open. That way folks could see that it was loaded but could not be fired. He reasoned that one day there could be a hold-up here and there would be no time to be loading guns. He would just need to snap the action closed and be ready to shoot. He always kept the gun ready when a strongbox was being loaded.'

'Did anyone else have access to the room?'

'It was never locked. Me and the two general hands, Nick Lister and Ike Baines, all had access to it but there was never a need to go in there. Marty Green worked at the stables, so he rarely came into the office.'

'I'd love to see Mawson's gun. Do you think you can find it?'

'I'll have a damn good try. I saw it after the shooting but then it seemed to have disappeared. It's probably around here someplace. What's on your mind, Pete?'

'I'm just gathering information at present. I need to know all that I can about what happened. Do you feel like a couple of beers after work if your wife will let you off the chain?'

'I'm not married now, Pete. My wife left me and moved to Chicago. She never liked living out here.'

'Sorry about that. Can you make it for a drink?'

Wilcox replied enthusiastically, 'Sure can. I'm so dry my hide's cracking.'

They had a couple of drinks, than parted company. Wilcox had introduced the deputy to a few more of the locals and Grey had dropped in to the saloon and spent a few minutes chatting before leaving to go home. As mayor, he was anxious to see how the new deputy was progressing.

Macgregor's store was not far from the coach office but was on the opposite side of the town's main street. His evening meal and the day's work behind him, Angus Macgregor was enjoying a smoke on the balcony above the store. It was part of his nightly ritual. His wife Mary and his daughter did not like the smell of his favourite pipe and had banished him to the balcony. Now in his late forties, Angus Macgregor was both large and strong. A reliable and law-abiding man, he had backed the town's late sheriff on occasions when the odds had been building up against the lawman. Those who knew him had a great respect for his ability both with a gun and his fists. He said little about his past but people knew that he had not always owned a general store. Some speculated that he had been a lawman at one time while others thought he might have spent time on the wrong side of the law. But all agreed that he was now a well-respected member of the community.

Locals who knew his habits often called greetings to him as they passed the store in the street. His large form bathed in the light of a lantern was a familiar sight as he leaned against a veranda post and idly looked down on the street below. The view offered little by way of entertainment because not much happened in Appsley on ordinary weeknights.

The streetlighting was poor and Mayor Grey had proved reluctant to authorize more public lamp sites. Consequently, much of the street's business was dark where premises had been closed for the night.

In one of these pools of darkness, between two now-empty buildings, a man with a rifle stood quietly. His eyes were fixed on the big man on the balcony about fifty yards away on the other side of the street. With the lamplight behind him, Macgregor was a plain target.

The man with the rifle looked up and down the street. He saw no one. Carefully he raised the Henry repeater to his shoulder and lined the sights on the storekeeper's broad body. He took a breath, held it and gently squeezed the trigger.

The rifle spat a tongue of flame from its muzzle and the report sounded like a cannon in the still night air.

The pipe spun from Macgregor's hand leaving a trail of sparks as it fell but its owner would never have noticed. The storekeeper was slammed back away from the rail to crumple in a heap on the veranda.

FOUR

Hewitt was making a final check on his animals when he heard the shot. It sounded fairly close. He turned and ran through the lane beside the sheriff's office to the main street. Other people were out too, looking up and down the street and speculating about where the shooter had been.

Then a loud female scream came from the balcony above the store.

Hewitt looked up and saw two women in the lamplight. One was kneeling and talking urgently to someone whom he could not see. The other was standing at the rail. 'Somebody get a doctor,' he heard Sue Macgregor call urgently. 'My father's been shot.'

A passer-by told the deputy. 'I know where Doc Robson is. I'll get him.'

'It's Deputy Hewitt,' he called up to the girl. 'A man's getting the doctor. Can you open the front door so that I can get in?'

A short time later Sue opened the door. Even in

the poor light, the deputy could see tears glistening on her cheeks. 'What happened, Miss Macgregor?'

'Pa's dead – someone shot him.'

'Did you see where the shot came from?'

She shook her head.' My mother and I were washing the dinner dishes – we only heard the shot.' At this point she broke down and sobbed again.

'We'd better go up and see your mother,' Hewitt said gently. 'Will you lead the way? It would be best to leave this door unlocked too. The doctor's coming.'

'There's nothing he can do,' Sue said tearfully. as she turned to lead the lawman to the stairs.

A glance at the fallen man showed that the girl had been right. He had been shot straight through the heart. Gently he helped the distraught, newly made widow to her feet. Macgregor's white shirtfront was soaked in blood but there were no signs of powder burns or a fallen weapon. The wound was not self-inflicted.

The doctor arrived then, a rotund little man of uncertain age, minus his coat and the celluloid collar he always wore. He had not wasted time getting to the scene but could only confirm what was already known.

'If you'll look after things here, Doctor. I'll make a few enquiries and try to find out what happened.' Hewitt was glad to quit the scene. He was never at home and always felt clumsy when trying to comfort grieving people.

'Does anyone know where that shot came from?'

he asked the onlookers who were gathering in the street outside the store. Nobody replied although there was great speculation among the crowd.

'No one would shoot Angus Macgregor on purpose,' a middle-aged lady said. 'He was such a gentleman.'

'It could have been an accident – some kid playing with a gun,' a man speculated.

'It was no accident,' another bystander announced. 'Angus made his share of enemies backing up the sheriff and helping him run the bad element out of this town. Looks like someone has decided to even the score.'

Hewitt searched between the buildings on the other side of the street and quickly came across the mouth of an alley that offered a good view of the Macgregors' balcony. Borrowing a lantern, he looked around for tracks. Unfortunately there were too many and he found nothing that proved the killer's presence there.

He asked around but nobody had seen anyone leave town. In the confusion that existed after the murder it would have been possible for someone to slip away but it seemed more likely that the killer was still in the town. Realizing that he was achieving nothing, he returned to the store.

The two women were still in shock. Doc Robson was handling the situation as well as it could be handled. 'I'll fix things as much as I can here,' he told Hewitt. 'There's little you can do. Get some rest and see me in the morning. By then I should know whether these ladies are up to being questioned. If I need you, I know where to find you.'

Hewitt thanked the doctor and left but he did not sleep very well that night. The murder – he was sure it was no accident – had seemed so brutal but the killer's motive had him puzzled. Was it connected with the strongbox robbery or was someone just settling an old score?

Alf Greer was supervising the harnessing of his coach team when the deputy found him next morning. After a brief introduction and a discussion about the weather, Hewitt asked the driver to recount what he had seen on the morning of the robbery.

Greer rubbed a stubbled chin and wrinkled his brow in thought. 'I didn't see a lot,' he admitted. 'All hell seemed to break loose. There was shootin' everywhere. I saw Sheriff Anderson get shot. Some jasper with a mask galloped up on a horse and downed him. Then the men holding my leaders let go their heads and the team bolted. It took nearly a quarter of a mile to get them pulled up – danged lucky the coach didn't turn over.'

'What can you tell me about the man who shot the sheriff?'

'Not much, he looked pretty ordinary. It ain't as if I had a lot of time to study him.'

'Anything unusual about the others?'

'I know a couple of them were ridin' quarter horses and there ain't a lot of them around these parts. They look awful big in the body compared to the mustangs that most ranches around here have. One was a liver chestnut, one was a bay but I can't recall seeing the third one. I figure they were counting on a quick getaway. Folks say there's nothing can get near one of them over a quarter-mile.'

'There's some might argue about that,' Hewitt commented. 'Do you know any ranch around here that has those quarter-milers?'

'Off hand I can't think of any but I'll ask around on my coach run. I might find out something.'

The deputy had one more question. 'Why do you think those bandits just started shooting instead of giving the guards a chance to surrender?'

Greer replied, 'Anyone who knew George Mawson or Ross Anderson would know that they wouldn't take a backward step for any bandit while they had guns in their hands. George had always let it be known that the first man who tried to rob his coach was going to get both barrels.' Fishing a large stem-winding watch from his vest pocket, the driver glanced at it and said, 'I have to get on the road now but I'll let you know if I find out anything useful.'

Hewitt walked away from the driver with the impression that a considerable amount of planning and inside information had gone into the recent outrage. Whoever the bandits were, someone in Appsley was working with them.

Angus Macgregor's murder might have been a

coincidence or it could have been connected but it was a complication that he did not need at such an early stage of enquiries.

FIVE

Hewitt had missed the funerals of Mawson and the sheriff but felt it was his duty to attend Macgregor's although he had not known the man. He stayed in the background but came forward after the ceremony to offer his condolences.

Both Sue and her mother were still badly shaken and he had intended to briefly pay his respects and depart. But Mary Macgregor retained her hold on his hand. Her red-rimmed eyes looked into Hewitt's and she said firmly, 'Please get the one who did this, Mr Hewitt. Promise me that.'

The 'getting' would be easier said than done and suddenly the deputy was on a spot. 'I can't give any guarantees, ma'am, but I will promise to do everything in my power to find that murderer.' He thought he saw a flicker of disappointment in the woman's eyes but knew that honesty was better than giving false hope. The absence of any leads or motives would make Macgregor's murder a difficult one to solve.

He spent the rest of the day asking questions around town. None of the other witnesses recalled anything special about the bandits' horses but he believed Greer. The man was a professional with horses and saw details that others might have missed.

Next morning he arose early and took Cactus out for a ride. He was a high-spirited animal that needed plenty of exercise. If he did not get enough he would arrange his own to the discomfort of a rider. The deputy was almost at the livery stable on the edge of town when a rider on a black horse emerged. It was Sue Macgregor.

She rode astride with a fringed divided shirt, a colourful blouse and a broad-brimmed black sombrero on her head, a pretty sight at any time but if anything she looked even more beautiful than at the first time he'd seen her.

The deputy raised his hat. 'Out for a morning ride, Miss Macgregor?'

'I am. I am trying to get life back to normal and it makes a good start to the day. I'll be out for about an hour. If you are not on business, I would be happy for a bit of company.'

Hewitt needed no second invitation. 'Cactus and I would enjoy having someone else to talk to.'

She smiled. 'Why is such a nice horse given a name like Cactus?'

'On account that he can be mighty hard to sit on. The cowhands on the ranch where he was raised christened him that. We had a few disagreements at first but things have settled down now.'

'He looks like a racehorse.'

'Not quite. He's three parts thoroughbred. His mother was half something else.'

'But I thought thoroughbreds would not stand up to Western work.'

'That breed can take a lot of work and is usually the first choice of cavalry officers. The ones raised here on the open range are acclimatized from birth and learn to pick up their feet. The Eastern-raised ones have a low galloping action and might be a bit faster. But on rough ground all horses need to step higher and those with the long, low stride can't use the advantage they might have on a race track.' As an afterthought the deputy continued, 'Speaking of fast horses, do you know of anyone around here who might have quarter-milers?'

'I can't say that I do but I'll ask Bob Cullinane at the livery stable. I heard him talking about them to a rancher the other day. They are becoming quite popular now. It seems that they are very quick off the mark and have enough weight to hold a big steer on a rope.'

Given the name, Hewitt could have asked the questions himself but the girl's offer had provided another excuse to see her again. He was enjoying the ride and the company but at the risk of touching a raw nerve, he could not quite forget why he was in Appsley. 'I'm sorry to ask you this but did your father make any special enemies around the town?' he asked.

'He did.'

The answer caught the lawman by surprise because to date he had only been told how popular Angus Macgregor had been. 'Do you know who they were?'

'Mostly I don't. Pa had been a deputy sheriff over in Kansas when he was young and had a lot of sympathy for Sheriff Anderson who was expected to keep order on his own. Sometimes, when it looked as though the sheriff was outnumbered by trouble-makers, he would take a hand. Mayor Grey and the town council always claimed there was not enough money to pay a deputy for Anderson, so Pa or Charley from the livery stable sometimes backed him up. The last clash he had was with the Count of No Account.'

Hewitt laughed. 'That's some title. Who is he?'

'He's a would-be gunman. A potential hired killer looking for someone to hire him. He has some unpronounceable Polish name and claims that his grandfather was a count in the old country. He was born here but likes to pretend he is European nobility. He likes the title of "the count" but nobody dares use the rest of the name. He is always talking about honour but would not know it if it jumped up and bit him. He tries to goad people into gunfights but they are always people who would not stand a chance against him. Pa and Sheriff Anderson did not subscribe to the count's code of honour. They ganged up on him and ran him out of town the last time he tried his tricks around here. '

'So the count had a grudge against both your father and the sheriff?'

'That's right. Being run out of town really hurt his pride.'

Hewitt looked at the sun climbing higher in the sky. 'I'll have to go to work now. I've really enjoyed this ride, Miss Macgregor.'

The girl flashed her white teeth in a smile. 'My name's Sue and I ride most mornings at six o'clock. You're welcome to come along at any time.'

'I'm mighty glad to hear that. My name's Pete or Peter if you prefer to be formal. Cactus needs the exercise and you are better company than he is, so I'll take you up on that offer as often as I can.'

After putting his horse away, Hewitt had breakfast and strolled across to the stage office. He found Wilcox at work doing the accounts. The manager was frowning as he studied an invoice. 'Howdy, John, you look worried.'

'It's just the price of horse feed. It's been going up gradually over the last couple of months. I'm glad I don't have to pay these bills.'

'You should have stuck to the railroad,' Hewitt told him. 'Trains don't need to be fed hay and grain.'

'They still need wood. But you're not here to discuss trains. What's on your mind?'

'What can you tell me about a character called "the count"?'

'He's a bad piece of work. Folks around here have

suspected him and some of his sidekicks of a couple of coach hold-ups but there's never been enough evidence to arrest him. If you ask me, he could well have been behind the recent killings, including the Macgregor murder. There was no love lost between him and Macgregor.'

'What does he do for a living?'

'He claims to be a gambler but no one in their right mind will gamble with him. If he loses, he claims that the winner was cheating and has shot a couple of people. I'm not sure how many he has killed but he seems to enjoy shooting folks.'

'Does he ride a quarter horse?'

'Not as far as I know,' Wilcox replied, 'but he changes horses regularly. To be honest, I'm not sure what sort of horse he rides. Horses are just horses to me and I don't take a lot of notice of them. Why do you ask?'

'Your driver, Greer, reckoned that at least two of the killers were riding quarter-milers. Do you remember anything about their horses?'

'Hell, Pete, I can't even recall seeing them. I was at the back of the building. I heard the shooting and ran to get a gun. As I came through I saw the coach go past the side window. By the time I got to the front door there was only dust and gun smoke in the air and bodies on the ground. It was one hell of a mess. At first I thought that all three had been killed. Young Ford was lucky to be alive.'

'I never did hear where the sheriff was shot. Was

he killed instantly?'

'I reckon so. The bullet hit him in the side of the head. It went straight through and left a big hole where it came out again. He was unlucky because a man on a galloping horse can't shoot too well with a six-shooter as a rule. Chances are that he shot for the biggest part of him and damn near missed. Anderson was dead unlucky. He was on foot with a rifle and should have won that shootout with no trouble but the bandit was lucky and really nailed him.'

Hewitt left the stage office and was intending to have another talk with the bank manager but as he passed Grey's office, he heard someone calling his name. He turned to see Veronica Cook waving from the office doorway.

'Deputy Hewitt, Mr Grey would like to see you when you have time.'

'There's no time like the present, Miss Cook. Lead the way.'

He found the mayor, as he'd expected he would be, sitting back in his big chair behind his highly polished desk. The lawyer wasted no time on pleasantries. 'You're just the man I wanted to see, Hewitt. Things seem to be getting out of hand around here. Have you made any progress on the robbery or the Macgregor murder?'

'I have a few ideas but nothing positive to back them up with yet. I think that Macgregor's killing is somehow linked to the robbery.'

'Nonsense,' Grey snorted. 'I suppose you'll tell me

next that Macgregor was part of the gang and was silenced for some reason or double-crossed by his partners in crime. It's obvious that the two events are not related and the more time you spend barking up the wrong tree, the further away the coach robbers get.'

'Not all the gang are far away. I reckon that at least one member is still in this town. And if I can find him, I might be able to make sense of this mess. Someone gave those bandits enough information for them to carry out a mighty slick raid.'

The mayor looked shocked. 'Don't tell me you believe the rumour going around that Basset might have helped rob his own bank.'

'I put no stock in rumours and have seen no reason to believe that particular one but someone who knew all the procedures planned that robbery. They knew that the coach was easier to hit in town where they had the complete element of surprise. They knew departure times and who was likely to be where. It was no bunch of out-of-work cowhands that planned this attack.'

'Most of the town knew when money was being shipped out. It was no great secret. Basset never advertised it but too many people were involved, bank staff and coach line staff. It could never be kept a secret. But I did not want to see you about bank procedures. The town council is being billed for your wages, and I am not sure that we are getting value for money.' Grey pointed a threatening finger at the deputy as he spoke. 'I expect to see some results for our money soon, or will want to know the reason why.'

'Be careful with that finger. It could be loaded,' Hewitt said casually as he turned and walked from the room.

SIX

Next morning the Count rode into Appsley. Neatly dressed, small, dark-haired, with a thin, carefully trimmed moustache, he resembled a professional man of some kind. But the image was marred by the big pair of Colts that he wore.

Hewitt saw him riding past and immediately recognized the type even though he had never known the man. It was a type that spelled trouble.

'It didn't take the.Count long to come back to Appsley.' Wilcox had joined Hewitt on the boardwalk. 'With Anderson and Macgregor out of the way, he's almost certain to try his luck with you. He's a nasty little skunk. Watch him, Pete.'

'I intend to. I'll be interested, too, in seeing who his friends are.'

'That's easy. The Bramley brothers, Elmer and Justin are friends of his. They have a ranch out on Prospector's Creek but they seem to know when their friend is in town. If he stays around, they'll join him

40

in a day or so.'

'Who are the Bramley brothers?'

'They're a couple of drunken no-goods, not very bright, brawlers and general nuisances. Their actions are more rash than rational, mainly due to a powerful kind of lunatic soup that they distil on their ranch and guzzle in large quantities. The story is that they are drinking their ranch out from under themselves and lately have taken to branding the wrong calves. Their neighbours are fast losing patience with them.'

'Do you think them capable of pulling off that coach robbery?'

Wilcox fiddled with his pipe for a while. 'I don't know,' he eventually replied. 'They're bad enough but probably not smart enough even when they are sober.'

'Sounds like things here could start to get a bit busy,' Hewitt observed, 'but I think I'll go to the store and have a word with Sue Macgregor.

'Keep your mind on your job,' Wilcox teased as he turned and walked back to his office.

Sue was serving a customer and while he waited for her to be finished, the deputy looked about. It was the usual frontier general store, selling food, clothing, footwear, patent medicines, tools, iron-mongery and ammunition.

He noted a few boxes of shotgun cartridges stacked on one of the back shelves. The boxes, slightly smaller than the others, were stacked at the far end of the shelf. A casual glance showed a sketch of a green cartridge on the label. His curiosity aroused, Hewitt looked closer. The printing announced that each box contained twenty-five twenty-gauge cartridges loaded with number six shot. They were suitable for ducks and small game but were only lethal to bigger targets at close range.

Sue was finished with her customer and greeted him with a friendly smile, but there was little joy in her face. He could see that painful memories were still returning to her among the familiar surroundings that had been so much of her father's life. In response to his question, she said that her mother was still feeling the shock of her husband's murder, and was not sufficiently recovered to resume her normal duties in the store.

Changing the subject, Hewitt asked, 'Did you happen to find any information about those quarter-milers?'

'Not a lot, but Bob Cullinane said he saw three men on quarter horses riding through town about three weeks ago. He said that they must have lived around the area because none had saddle-bags such as travellers would be using. He didn't recognize the riders but thinks that they might have been from one of the local ranches.'

'I notice that you have some twenty-gauge cartridges there. Do you sell many?'

Sue shook her head. 'No. Most shotguns around here are ten-gauge or twelve-gauge. We've had those four boxes of twenty-gauge there for ages. Pa got them in for Max Bramley; he apparently had a twenty-gauge that he used for snakes. Max died a bit over a year ago. His two sons have the ranch now.'

'There are only three boxes of those cartridges on the shelf,' Hewitt said.

Sue glanced at the shelf again. 'You're right. Pa must have sold one of them.'

'Would you have any idea who might have bought them?'

'If one of the ranches that have accounts bought it there would be a record, but there would be none for a cash sale. Is it important?'

'It could be but I'm not sure,' the deputy admitted. 'I would appreciate it if you would look back through some of your recent accounts to see if you have a record of its sale. But don't tell anyone.'

'Do you think this box of cartridges could have anything to do with my father's murder?' Sue made no attempt to disguise the concern in her voice.

'It's possible. I also think that the killer is still around, so for safety's sake, tell nobody about this.'

'I saw the Count back in town,' Sue said. 'He would not have dared show his face if my father was still around. Are you going to run him out of town again?'

'Not unless I have to. He's the sort of character I like to keep my eye on. If he's up to something, I would like to know about it.'

'It's possible that he murdered my father. He had

a grudge against him and could have crept into town, shot him and got out again. He knows this area fairly well.'

'We certainly can't rule out the Count. He's one of a few who have to be considered. I'd better let you get back to work. Will you be riding in the morning?'

'I hope to.'

'If all goes well I'll join you. Remember, not a word to anyone about those cartridges.'

The sun was higher and the day seemed hotter when Hewitt emerged from the shade of Macgregor's store. He squinted along the street and saw a couple of horses hitched outside the saloon and a dog scratching itself as it lay in the shade of a building. An elderly lady driving a buggy turned into the street but otherwise it was deserted.

He saw Wilcox then, standing in the doorway of the coach office. The stageline manager waved to attract his attention. His curiosity aroused, the deputy crossed the street to where his friend waited. 'What's worrying you, John?'

Glancing toward the saloon as though fearful of being seen, Wilcox replied, 'I thought you might like to know. The two Bramleys are in town. They're over in the saloon now with the Count. Be careful of them. Unless I miss my guess, they'll be full of Dutch courage and will try you out soon just to see what they can get away with. If you have to take them on, I'll back you up although I'm not the world's best shot.'

'That makes two of us,' Hewitt said grimly. 'I was hoping that I might have a chance to study these characters before having to confront them. I might see if I can head off any trouble before it gets started. I'm hoping I might be able to find out a few things without resorting to gunplay.'

'I don't like your chances, but good luck. If I hear shots, I'll come running.'

SEVEN

Hewitt loosened his revolver in its holster and hoped that his nervousness was not showing before he pushed his way through the batwing doors of the saloon. He glanced around. It was a working day and there were few customers.

Two men who looked like teamsters were seated at one table talking quietly together. The Count, and two large, rough-looking men dressed as cowhands were seated on the other side of the room. Both were unshaven and their worn clothing obviously had not seen too many wash tubs. At first glance the scene was peaceful enough but the deputy noticed two ominous signs immediately; the three men were silent and the bartender was looking decidedly nervous.

'Having a quiet day, Phil?'

'I am, Pete and I would greatly appreciate it if it stays that way. You probably don't know but that's the Count and the Bramley brothers sitting at that table over there and they don't like lawmen. If looks could kill, you'd be dead already. Tread very carefully.'

'I always do,' Hewitt said quietly as he turned and strolled over to the trio at the table.

They watched him with hostility and suspicion showing in their faces.

'Howdy, gents. I'm Pete Hewitt, filling in as sheriff. Are you just passing through?'

Justin Bramley, the elder of the brothers, glared at the lawman with bloodshot eyes from beneath bushy eyebrows, contempt showing on a face that bore more than one sign of a physical disagreement. 'No, we ain't just passing through. My brother and I live here and will be here long after you're gone.'

'You're probably right,' Hewitt said casually. 'I'm still getting to know the locals here.' He turned to Elmer Bramley, who bore a striking resemblance to his brother and had a similar scowl on his face. 'I suppose there are no prizes for guessing that you two are brothers.'

'You're dead right,' Elmer confirmed.

The Count was next to be questioned. 'That leaves you. You don't look like a rancher to me.'

'How very perceptive,' the Count said sarcastically. 'I suppose there is some reason behind this intrusion on our privacy but I have nothing to hide. Folks around here call me the Count. I'm a gambler and I visit this place periodically looking for suckers to fleece. I'm breaking no law, so run away now, sonny.'

Hewitt gave a slight smile as though embarrassed. 'I'm afraid it's not as easy as that. Some people around here have been killed and a strongbox taken, so I am rather interested in the comings and goings of a few people, namely, you three.'

Then suddenly the deputy's gun was in his hand. Caught unprepared and still seated and hampered by the table, the others had no chance to draw their own weapons. Momentarily panic showed in their eyes, but then reason took over and they placed their hands on the table.

Keeping all three under his gaze, Hewitt told them, 'Now you can answer my questions here or over in the calaboose – or if anyone feels lucky you might care to go for a gun. There's just a chance that one of you might put a bullet in me before I kill all three of you. Make up your minds.'

Justin Bramley was the first to reach a decision. He was closest, came out of his chair and instantly threw himself at the lawman. Almost as though he had been rehearsing the move, Hewitt slammed the gun barrel against the side of the big man's head and dropped him into the sawdust on the floor. 'Don't!' he warned the others who were about to take advantage of the diversion. Sullenly they raised their hands.

The lawman plucked the gun from Justin's holster and tucked it in his belt as the dazed rancher struggled to all fours. 'Now gents, undo those gun belts and put your guns on the table. Be mighty careful how you do it, because at this stage it won't take much to make me shoot.'

Hate blazed from the Count's dark eyes, for he had little choice but to obey. 'You're a sneaky back-shooting skunk,' he snarled. 'If you were a real man you'd be prepared to face me out in the street. You don't have the guts of a rabbit.'

As he carefully picked up the revolvers and started stuffing them in his belt, the lawman said, 'I'm not too enthusiastic about giving people chances to kill me. As you just found out, I cheat. Now, are we going to have a conversation here or over at my office? If I have to march you across the street, none of you will be getting out again until I get all the right answers.'

Surprisingly, the Count suddenly seemed co-operative. 'I suppose you want to know where we were when the coach was robbed.'

'That's a good point to start.'

The Count casually took a cigar from a silver case, bit off the end and lit it. 'Be so kind as to refresh my memory. What date was that?'

'It was the twenty-second of May.'

Exhaling a cloud of smoke in the lawman's general direction, the gambler said, 'I was a hundred miles away riding a string of good luck at Powell's Junction. Plenty of poorer but wiser citizens of that fair town can vouch for that. The sheriff was watching me very closely and a telegraph message to him should verify what I am saying.'

'What about you?' Hewitt demanded of Elmer Bramley.

The rancher looked puzzled and frowned as he tried to recall the day. At last he mumbled, 'I ain't sure but me and Justin spend most of our time at the ranch. That's where we would have been.'

'Did any of your neighbours see you there?'

'You can bet they did. Them sneaky sonsofbitches watch us all the time. They reckon we're rustlers. Mullane and his men would say anything to bring trouble on us.'

'Who's Mullane?'

'Clint Mullane. He bought Green's TG spread last year. He don't like us at all.'

'Good taste is no crime,' Hewitt reminded him.

Justin said angrily, 'Don't believe anything Mullane tells you. He'd lie real quick to get us into trouble.'

'I suppose you'll be riding out to the TG now,' Elmer said, 'just to hear a few more lies about us.'

'I suppose you have heard the rumour that Basset might have masterminded the robbery himself,' the Count said smoothly. 'The dogs are barking that someone on the inside planned that robbery.'

'When I can find a dog that talks, I'll ask him what he knows. Meanwhile I'll keep an open mind. As long as you gents don't cause any trouble, you can stay in town.'

'What about our guns?' Justin growled.

'You can collect them as you leave town. Don't try anything silly like trying to get others.'

The Count took another draw on his cigar and

glared coldly at the lawman. 'I won't forget this, Hewitt. You have insulted my integrity and some day you will have to face me for that. Honour demands it.'

'Let me tell you now, Count. I don't worry about honour. I'm sneaky and I cheat. If you cause a situation where I have to kill you. I will load the dice in my favour any way I can.'

'I'd expect no less from your type,' the Count said grandly as the lawman walked away.

EIGHT

The new day was looking good and it improved even more in Hewitt's mind when he saw Sue waiting on her black pony outside the livery stable. She smiled and gave a cheery greeting as she turned her mount alongside Cactus. 'Do you wish to ride in any special direction?' she asked.

'I wouldn't mind riding out towards the Bramley ranch if it suits you, Sue.'

'Sounds fine to me but we would never be able to get anywhere near the ranch in the time we have. It's about twenty miles away. The scenery's not bad though, so it's a good direction to ride.'

Hewitt looked at his companion. 'The scenery's not too bad right here.'

Sue laughed. 'Thank you. You are very flattering this morning. Have you been taking lessons from the Count?'

'The Count couldn't teach pigs to be dirty. Don't spoil the day by even mentioning him.'

They followed the coach road varying the pace according to the ground they were on at the time. The land sloped upwards to a long ridge that dominated the landscape surrounding the town and afforded a panoramic view of the countryside. As the climb was a fairly steep one they halted on the summit to allow the horses a short rest.

It was Sue who first spotted the other riders.

'Look along the ridge to the left,' she said as she pointed. 'Someone else is out for an early morning ride.'

Three horsemen had halted about a quarter of a mile away and were looking down on the town. Then one dismounted and passed his horse's reins to the nearest mounted man. Sunlight flashed on bright metal and the watchers realized that the man on foot was using a brass telescope.

'I wonder what they're up to,' Hewitt said. Something about the strangers made him uneasy. 'I could understand men looking for game or even strayed stock but they're unlikely to be down there in the streets of Appsley.'

The barrel of the telescope flashed again as the man using it changed position. 'They've seen us,' Hewitt said. 'He's looking straight at us.'

For a couple of seconds the man with the telescope watched them. Then he turned and mounted his horse. The three riders wheeled their animals and trotted down a spur of the ridge. Soon they were out of sight.

'They look like men who prefer not to be seen,' Hewitt observed. 'I wonder what they were up to.'

'I don't know,' Sue replied, 'but I'm glad they were not too close to us. I don't think that they were just out enjoying the morning air.'

'I agree. Chances are that they know who we are but I would dearly love to know who those three were. They looked like they were up to no good.'

The ride back to town seemed all too short but both knew they had a busy day ahead and could not afford to stay away from their work any longer. After tentatively agreeing to meet for another ride in two days' time, the girl and the lawman parted company at the livery stable.

Hewitt fed and groomed Cactus, had his own breakfast and had just opened the office door when he had a visitor. John Grey came through the door, his face flushed with anger. 'I want a word with you, Hewitt.'

The deputy indicated a chair near his desk. 'Go ahead.'

The mayor preferred to remain standing. 'The Count's still in town. What are you doing about him? The Bramleys are with him too. We don't want people like that in Appsley.'

'As long as they stay within the law, I'm prepared to let them be here. If you look you'll see that they have no guns. I have them here.'

Grey gave an angry snort. 'That type always carry hideout guns or knives. You're a fool if you think you have disarmed them. I want them out of town.'

'That's too bad because I want them here where I can watch them for a while. If they break the law, I'll have to act but while they are being good boys, it suits me to have them here.'

'Well, it doesn't suit me. Might I remind you that I am paying your wages. I can fire you.'

'The county sheriff pays my wages and he bills you for my services. He sent me here and he's the one who will tell me when to leave. You can write to him or maybe send a telegraph message if you're not happy but until I hear from him I stay where I am. Bit by bit I am picking up pieces of information and I'm starting to get a few answers.'

'What have you found out?'

'I'll tell you when I start arresting people.'

'You won't be here long enough to arrest anyone. I'll make an official complaint. You're going, Hewitt.'

The deputy leaned back in his chair and fixed Grey with a hard look. 'I'm not sure,' he said, 'whether you are just an interfering busybody, or you really don't want this robbery and murder to be cleared up.'

Spluttering with rage, Grey turned and stormed out.

Hewitt arose and made his way down to the coach station. He waved to Wilcox as he passed his office window but went down the side of the building to the corrals and sheds, where spare equipment was stored. He wanted to ask a few questions of the two stable hands, Nick Lester and Ike Baines.

Lister was a tubby little man, with a round, cheerful face. He had lived in Appsley most of his life except for a few years in the East during the Civil War. He had no hesitation in giving his version of the robbery. 'I thought I was back at Gettysburg. There were guns going off everywhere and the sound was echoing off the buildings. Those bandits sure threw a lot of lead around.'

Baines was much younger and thinner than his co-worker but heartily endorsed what the other had said. 'That's right. I ain't never been in a gunfight before and without a gun it was mighty scary. When George's shotgun blew up, it sounded like the end of the world. Even if I had a gun, I ain't sure I would have hung around any longer.'

The mention of the shotgun jogged Hewitt's memory. 'Do you know what happened that gun?'

'Sure we do,' Lister said. He pointed to a barrel in the corner of the stable. 'It's over there with the trash. The butt's missing. It wasn't damaged and I gave it to Otto Hinkler down the road. He thinks he can replace a broken stock on his gun with it. The rest of the gun is a total wreck.'

Hewitt walked to the barrel and looked inside. He quickly extracted the mangled remains of twin barrels and a badly damaged firing mechanism. The connecting rib between the two barrels had torn loose from its welds and was twisted out of position. Some of the spiral welds peculiar to Damascus barrels had also opened. Large sections of both barrels were missing, leaving jagged holes in the steel. 'There must have been bits of this gun flying everywhere,' he said as he examined the barrels.

'Probably,' Lister agreed, 'but a hell of a lot of it finished up in George's face. It made a real mess of him.'

As he examined the barrels the deputy noted a tiny fragment of green paper caught on the jagged edge of a blown-out section. It confirmed what he had been beginning to guess, but he dared not say anything. Instead, he concealed his excitement and announced that he was taking the barrels as evidence.

Thanking the pair he left the stables and walked back along the alley. Pausing briefly outside Wilcox's open window, he looked in. The manager put down his pen when he saw the deputy. 'Did you learn anything new from the stable hands?'

'I'm not sure yet. Will you be having a beer after work tonight?'

'I will if I can get this paper work out of the way. I should be there about five-thirty or so.'

Hewitt had not been long back in his office when he heard horses outside the door and boots on the boardwalk. Then the Count and the Bramleys strolled through the door. They looked sullen and an aura of danger seemed to hang about them. 'We're here for our guns,' the Count announced.

'Are you leaving town?'

'We are. We kept our part of the deal. I had a good night at the cards last night so I'm having a couple of days at the Bramley ranch before I move on.'

'Glad to hear it,' Hewitt said as he unlocked a desk drawer. He passed over the four weapons he had confiscated the night before.

The Bramleys dropped theirs into their empty holsters. The Count put one gun away but he glanced at the cylinder of the other and could see that it was loaded. The dark eyes narrowed but he did not holster the gun. 'You're getting careless, Hewitt,' he said. 'If I wasn't a gentleman, I could kill you right now.'

The deputy seemed unconcerned. 'Don't try it, Count. Remember I told you that I cheat.'

The Count gave a wintry smile as he dropped the weapon back in its holster. 'You probably do but you can't dodge me for ever. Some day we will meet and see who is the better man.'

'Gunfights only prove that one man was a better shot than the other, or was luckier. They don't prove the true worth of a man.'

'We'll debate that point again soon,' the Count threatened. He would have turned away to leave but Hewitt halted him. He reached into a desk drawer and produced eight .45 cartridges. 'These belong to you and your friends,' he said as he passed them over. 'I took them out of the cylinders of your guns. If you had cocked any gun to fire, the hammer would only fall on an empty chamber and the one behind it was empty too. You would have needed to cock your guns and pull the triggers twice before you could fire a shot. I would not have given you time for that.'

For a second the Count looked surprised as he took the cartridges but then he swore softly and added, 'You're right, Hewitt. You are a cheating sonofabitch. We'll meet again. You'll run out of tricks before I run out of patience.'

NINE

Hewitt rose very early next morning and rode back to the ridge where he had seen the three riders. This time he had a pair of field glasses in a leather case slung from his saddle horn.

Tracks and old cigarette butts showed that the place had been visited regularly and that the visitors had waited around, though for what reason he could only guess. It could only have been an observation post of some kind but what had the strangers been watching? He dismounted and swept the field glasses over the town below.

He could see the back of the bank and Macgregor's store. A slight change of direction showed the front of the coach station and the alley beside it. He could even see the window of Wilcox's office. Another slight change of direction showed the rear of the brown-painted building where Grey had his office. Still none the wiser, he returned the glasses to their case and mounted Cactus.

The regular comings and goings had made a beaten path so the deputy turned his mount along it. At first it led down the reverse slope of the hill and it was easy to follow, but then it went into a pine thicket and the carpet of fallen needles partly obscured it. A few minutes of riding about were necessary before Hewitt was satisfied that he was on the trail again. The country became steeper and he found himself going around the side of a hill with a small spring bubbling out of a tangle of vines some distance below him. Another mile and the spring had become a creek. The country was opening out too and changing from rocky ridges to open grasslands. Miles away in the distance he saw two separate columns of smoke rising against the cloudless blue sky. He surmised that it was ranch houses with breakfast cooking and knew that the buildings would not be as close together as they appeared to be in the distance.

It seemed likely that the mysterious riders had come from one of those ranches but time was running out. Reluctantly the deputy turned his mount homewards. He would ask around Appsley and find out a bit more about the ownership of the ranches in question.

Willie Freeman was lucky. He saw Hewitt's horse's bright chestnut coat showing through a patch of dark green pine seedlings and quickly reined his horse behind a large boulder. Had he emerged from cover a second earlier, it was possible that Hewitt would have seen him. He recognized the horse because he had seen it close up through a telescope, the previous day. To his relief he saw the deputy change course and start riding back the way he had come. But the presence of a lawman on the rarely-used trail did little for his peace of mind.

The heavily built gunman scratched his short brown beard as if seeking inspiration and eventually decided that it was more important to warn his companions. If there was a message from their man in town, it would have to wait.

As soon as the deputy was a safe distance away, Freeman turned his horse and rode back to the ranch as quickly as the rough ground would allow.

When Hewitt reached town, he followed his usual routine of caring for his horse and then having breakfast. When this was over, the store was open and he strolled across the street to it.

Sue looked up when he entered and flashed him a welcoming smile. 'You're out early today, Pete. Is this business or a social call?'

'I'm afraid it's business. Did you have any luck in finding who bought those twenty-gauge cartridges?'

'Unfortunately there's no record in the ranch accounts so that means it was a cash sale. Ma knows nothing about it so my father must have sold it. How important is it to find out?'

'I think it could be very important but at this stage it's safest for you if I don't tell you of my suspicions. Don't mention those cartridges to anyone. I won't be riding in the morning and it might be an idea if you don't ride for a while in that last direction we took. I had a look up there this morning. Those three characters have been coming there regularly and I'm not sure what they are up to. I found a little creek up there and saw two ranches away to the south-east. Would you know what ranches they are?'

'They could be Bramleys' and the TG ranch but I'm not sure. They are over that way somewhere.'

'Do you know anyone with a map?'

'Yes, John Grey has one in his office. As a lawyer he handles all the land deals around here.'

Hewitt smiled ruefully. 'Grey and I are not on the best of terms. Do you know anyone else?'

'Mr Basset at the bank might have one. He has a lot of mortgages on the local ranches.'

'Thanks. I'll try him first. He might be slightly higher than Grey on the sociability scale at present. I'd better get back to the less enjoyable aspect of my work now.'

The banker was not pleased to see the deputy and pretended to be busier than he was just to keep Hewitt waiting for a while. Eventually he condescended to see Hewitt. 'Be brief,' he snapped. 'I'm a very busy man.'

The lawman enquired about a map and it seemed to him that Basset was rather happy to tell him that he could not help. But refusing to be dismissed so quickly, Hewitt asked, 'How often do you get transfers of money coming through here on the coach?'

'For safety reasons, I'm not sure I should tell you that. Those transfers are the bank's business.'

'The bank's last piece of business got two men killed and one of your employees badly injured, so I reckon things got a bit sloppy from a safety point of view.'

'That won't happen again. Bandits won't try the same trick twice and I have requested that next time there will be two guards with the money.'

'While I am here, I would appreciate advice about big cash shipments coming through.'

Basset gave the slightest hint of a smile. 'You need not worry, Deputy Hewitt, because I don't think that you will be here for long. Good day to you.'

A pleasant surprise awaited Hewitt when he reached Grey's office. Veronica Cook explained that the lawyer had been called suddenly to visit a client out on a ranch. She also confirmed that Grey had the sort of map that the deputy needed. It was hanging on his office wall and she allowed him to see it. Names had been pencilled in at various places and the ranch that Hewitt thought would have been the closest of those he had seen, had the name Green crossed out and Mullane written underneath. He figured that the next one would be the Bramley ranch. Both ranches appeared to be on the eastern bank of Prospector's Creek, the stream that Hewitt had followed for a short distance. It wound across the flat land below in a series of big loops like the track of a giant snake, and along its length smaller tributaries fed into it.

The map showed a road going to the ranches but it detoured a long way to the south because the hills east of Appsley were too steep for wheeled vehicles. By road both ranches were twenty miles or more from town, but in a straight line over the ridges they were only about half that distance.

Hewitt had seen what he wanted and thanked the lady as he left the office. 'I was not sure that your boss would have been so helpful. Him and I had a few words the other day.'

The lady laughed. 'Don't worry, Deputy. John has a big idea of his own importance and likes to throw his weight around but he's not a vindictive man. He can be very nice with people he likes.'

'That doesn't help me because I seem to be one of the people he doesn't like. But your help is much appreciated.'

'Are you getting any closer to those who killed the sheriff and George Mawson?'

'I'm picking up a few bits of information here and there but I'm a long way from finding out exactly who did it. The picture is becoming clearer but I need to know a lot more yet.'

Hewitt's next call was at the coach company office. Wilcox was busy as the coach was due to go out the following morning. 'I might not be able to get over to the saloon tonight,' he said. 'I have to get things organized for tomorrow. Have you made any progress?'

'I'm not sure,' Hewitt answered. 'A few more details will need to be checked out. I'd like to find just where the Count and the two Bramleys fit into things and I have the feeling that something else is being planned. I have tried to get Basset to increase the guards on any future money shipments through here but he's mighty stubborn.'

'Our coach line will pay for one guard but the banks will have to pay for the other one. They are a miserable lot and don't like paying for anything that might never be used.'

'This town and your coaches are targets whenever those inter-bank shipments of money are coming through.'

Wilcox said in disbelief, 'Surely they don't expect that they'd get away with another surprise attack like the last one. They would be far safer out in the brush stopping the coach, possibly after picking off the guard with a rifle.' He paused and then asked, 'Just on that subject, are you any closer to finding out who shot Macgregor?'

'I think I know why he was killed and it should give me a good idea as to who needed him dead.'

'Can you tell me?'

'Not at this stage. Too many wild stories fly around this town. Basset is rather upset by the rumour that he may have been involved in robbing his own bank and I can't say that I blame him. Unfortunately, he's so annoyed that I am not likely to get much co-operation from him.'

'He's always annoyed.' Wilcox chuckled. 'He has all the charm of a rattlesnake and is totally heartless in matters of money. People don't like him and make no secret of it.' Then he changed the subject. 'I saw that you found the barrels of Mawson's gun. It sure was a mess, wasn't it?'

'One of your stable hands tossed it in a trash barrel. That Damascus steel made a pretty pattern on the barrel but apparently it didn't stand up too well to heavy charges. Has your company replaced the guard's gun yet?'

'Yes, a new Winchester gun arrived the other day. They have had some good ones specially made up in England and just put their name on them.'

'Look after it,' Hewitt said seriously, 'because I reckon it might be needed soon.'

TEN

Clint Mullane tore open the envelope that he found in the TG ranch mailbox. He recognized the handwriting even though the brief note inside it was unsigned.

Arthur Turner was seated at the meal table nearby shovelling breakfast into his mouth. 'You look worried, Clint. Word from town again?'

'That's right. It's that new deputy. He's getting too nosy. We thought he'd just keep the seat warm for the next sheriff, but instead he's starting to act like a full-time lawman.'

Between mouthfuls Turner agreed. 'That's why Willie saw him hanging about on the back trail to town. He knows something or he wouldn't be there.'

'He saw us the other day and that's what made him suspicious. He's probably watching that ridge now and has maybe figured that we are looking for signals from town. That sort of complicates things. How are we going to know about the next money shipment when it's not safe to look for signals?'

'There's only one way to make it safe and that's to get rid of Deputy Hewitt.'

Turner was not so sure. 'The law's likely to take things a mite seriously if a second lawman gets killed in Appsley in such a short time.'

'I have an idea about that but I'll need to see the boss before I start it going.'

'You know he don't like us being seen in town too often. We're supposed to be hard-working cowmen who only come to town on paydays.'

'Don't worry. It will be dark by the time I get to town. I'll see the boss and be home again by morning. Nobody need see me.'

That morning Sue and Hewitt had ridden out to the west of the town. The deputy had his field glasses with him and they halted at a vantage point overlooking the town. He dismounted and carefully studied the ridge on the eastern side. There was no sign of life. 'Looks like our friends with the telescope are not there today.'

'We could be at the wrong time,' Sue suggested. 'They might not come at the same time every day.'

'You're probably right.' He stepped into the stirrup as he spoke and swung back on to Cactus. 'It's time I was on my way back to work. It would be nice if for just one day we could take our time and stay out as long as we felt like it.'

They returned to town and went their separate

ways. Doubts were nagging at Hewitt and he asked a few more questions around Appsley in an attempt to obtain a clear picture of what had occurred leading up to the raid. He found an old friend of Sheriff Anderson's who told him that he had shared drinks with the two dead men on the previous night. They had spent about an hour together but neither man had drunk heavily.

He made another stop at the coach office and found Wilcox in a rare idle moment. He looked up from the newspaper he was reading when the lawman entered. 'You're looking mighty serious today, Pete. What have you been up to?'

'Nothing much, just trying to fit a few pieces into the puzzle or maybe puzzles if the Macgregor murder is not connected to the robbery.'

'Do you really think the two events are connected? I wouldn't be looking much further than the Count for Macgregor's shooting. He had a grudge against him.'

The lawman looked doubtful and his forehead wrinkled in a frown. 'I'm not so sure. It doesn't seem the Count's style. He wants people to know who he has killed. I checked on his story that he could not have been involved in the robbery and he's clear on that score.'

'But you're assuming that the killings are connected. The Count is as treacherous as they come. Don't be fooled by that gentleman act that he puts on. Under that he is a very nasty little killer.'

'I heard that Mawson and Anderson were in the saloon together the night before the raid. Do you know if that's right?'

Wilcox nodded. 'It seems likely. But I wouldn't know. I was down at the stables for quite a while that night with Lister and Bathes. We had to order some more fodder for the teams and I was working out how much would be needed. Neither of those boys had much schooling and it took me a long time to work out what our monthly requirements would be.'

'So the office was unattended for a while?'

'That's right. But we have a secure room to lock up baggage and valuables and I knew that George Mawson would not be long away. He liked to turn in early on nights before long runs.'

'Was the guard's room locked?'

'No need. There was only a bunk and some blankets. Nobody would want to steal them.'

'There was also a shotgun and ammunition, wasn't there?'

'You're right,' Wilcox admitted. 'I forgot about that. It might have been better for George if someone had stolen that damned death trap.'

'When is the next coach due?'

'It's a twice-weekly service, arrives here tomorrow night and leaves the following morning. There is no strongbox on this one and no passengers booked to leave from here, so I could have an easy time for a change.'

But Hewitt would have little leisure that night.

He had finished his evening meal and was thinking of closing the sheriff's office for the night when he noticed a man dismounting in front of the saloon. The Count was back in town. He knew then that trouble was not far away. Ensuring that his Winchester carbine was fully loaded, he sat back in the office and waited.

An hour dragged by and then Baines, the stable hand, came in from the saloon. 'I thought you'd like to know, Pete. There's a gun fight on the way. Gopher Doherty has just challenged the Count. They're gonna shoot it out in the street.'

'Who's this Gopher character?' Hewitt asked as he came out of his chair and grabbed his Winchester.

'He's a little red-headed runt who goes looking for fights every time he gets a few drinks aboard. Usually he only gets into fist fights but the Count only fights one way. Gopher doesn't have a chance but he's too drunk to know it.'

The deputy levered a cartridge into the breech of his rifle, put the hammer on half cock and stepped into the street. Two men were already out there, standing about thirty yards apart. Onlookers were mostly viewing from the saloon windows and doors because stray bullets could be expected on the street. In his current state, none expected much accuracy from Gopher.

The Count had swept back his coat and stood with both hands poised over the butts of his twin guns, ready to draw and shoot at the first suspicious move his opponent made.

'Count!' Hewitt called. 'Hold your fire.'

'Get out of the way, Hewitt. This little coyote challenged me and I have never ignored a challenge yet.'

'Yeah, stay outa this,' Doherty mumbled. 'This is our fight.'

With no time for argument the deputy walked up to Gopher, used his rifle barrel to swat the man's hand away from his gun, and plucked the weapon from its holster. The drunk yelped in protest and waved his injured hand but Hewitt had already forgotten him. He turned to the Count. 'This affair's over. I'll take this character to the calaboose to sober up.'

'I'll say when it's over,' the other snarled. 'I'm the injured party here and that little runt is as good as dead.'

'He's out of the fight. There's no honour in shooting drunks. Go back into the saloon and forget this.'

'I'm not forgetting anything, Hewitt. You just took this yellow coyote's place. Go for your gun any time you feel like it. Nobody takes my guns and lives.'

'Think it over, Count. I already have a gun in my hand and you won't beat me to the draw. Over this distance you might manage to hit me with a revolver but it's an easy shot for someone with a rifle. You're a gambler, so start figuring your chances. The deck's stacked against you. Now I'm going to give you three options; first you can go for your guns but I wouldn't advise it. The second choice is to drop your guns on the ground and go back to your cards and collect your guns when you leave town. The third choice is to keep your guns, get on your horse right now and leave town.'

'You're yellow, Hewitt. Too scared to face a man on equal terms. But I'm better than you any day of the week.'

'Make up your mind, Count. I don't want to kill you but I will if you even look like giving me trouble. What's it to be?'

The Count's eyes darted about as if seeking a way out of his problem and his tongue suddenly flicked over his dry lips. He knew that the odds were against him. At last he shrugged his shoulders. 'There'll be other times, Hewitt. I'll leave town now but next time I see you I intend to kill you.'

'Thanks for the warning,' Hewitt called. 'Now I'll give you one. If I see you in this town again, I'll shoot you on sight.' He watched closely as the Count walked to the nearby hitching rail. It hurt the gunman's pride to back down before an audience and there was still the chance that he would try some trick.

As the Count mounted his horse, Doherty found his voice again. 'And don't come back,' he yelled drunkenly, 'or I'll give you more of the same.

The gunman turned his horse and glared at the two men in the street. 'I'll come back and when I do, you pair are dead men.'

ELEVEN

Hewitt escorted Gopher to his office and lodged him in one of the cells. He was not in the best of moods. A prisoner meant that he had to stay to watch him but it also meant that the Count knew right where to find them if he decided to double back. He drew the blinds on the office windows. There was no sense in giving an unseen gunman an easy shot. For safety's sake he also put out one of the office lamps; no point in being a brightly lit target.

One by one the lamps in Appsley went out as the townspeople sought their beds. The deputy was about to settle down on a bunk behind the main office when he heard something clink against metal. The sound was coming from the cell area. He was on his feet when a gunshot exploded. The noise, magnified by the confined space, sounded like the report of a cannon.

Grabbing his gun, Hewitt ran through the connecting door. Much to his relief Gopher was on

75

his feet but looking at the window, high up in the cell wall. 'What in the hell was that?' he mumbled.

The lawman knew only too well what it was and ran to the back door of the premises. Just as he threw open the door, it occurred to him that the first shot had only been a decoy, to lure him outside. He threw himself flat.

An unseen gunman fired and the bright muzzle flash came from the shadows near the corner of an adjoining building. A bullet tore splinters from the doorjamb just above Hewitt's head. He triggered a quick shot in reply though, in the darkness, he was unlikely to score a hit. It was intended to discourage any further attack and to that end it succeeded. Seconds later he heard a horse. In a clatter of hoofs, the rider fled into the night.

The deputy knew that pursuit would be useless and, if anything, might even lure him into another ambush. He replaced the fired shell in his gun and after closing the door behind him, returned to Gopher in the cell.

The shooting had shocked him into a state that was almost sober. He looked relieved when the deputy came through the door. Uncertain of the outcome of the gun fight, he half-expected to see the Count.

'What happened, Gopher?'

'How would I know? One minute I was havin' a nice sleep and then it seemed the whole world exploded.'

'You didn't hear anything?'

'Not a damned thing.' As he spoke, Gopher suddenly clasped his head and twisted his face in pain. 'I can hear something now, though, sounds like someone hammerin'. Are you sure I ain't been shot in the head?'

'No such luck. Now go back to sleep. I'll let you out in the morning if you behave.'

As he tried to sleep later, Hewitt went over the night's happenings in his mind. Something was not as it seemed.

He found evidence of his suspicions the next day. The bullet fired into the cell had gone through the roof. It had never been intended to harm Gopher because the shooter would not be able to reach the window and fire down into the cell. It had been a ruse to lure the deputy outside.

After releasing a sick and penitent prisoner, Hewitt went outside and looked around the building. The tracks showed where a horseman had ridden to the cell window, reached up and fired through the bars. The horse tracks then led into the street where he would be unable to follow them further because early risers had partially obliterated them as they went about the town. He saw enough though to know that the rider was heading for the southern end of town.

The bullet that clipped the doorjamb had continued on to lodge in one of the office's interior walls. Its low-angled path showed that a man on horseback could not have fired it. Hewitt walked to the building that had sheltered the gunman and saw where his would-be killer had hidden around the corner. The prints of flat-heeled townsman's boots showed clearly in the dust. The Count wore high-heeled riding boots. Two men had been involved in the failed ambush.

The shooting had not gone unnoticed and several people, when they met the deputy, asked what had happened. The general opinion was that the Count had returned so he made no attempt to say otherwise. But Hewitt knew that only one of the would-be killers had left town.

Later in the morning he paid a call on Grey. As he was mayor of the town, the deputy thought it best to keep him reasonably informed. The lawyer was not pleased to see him.

'I hear you had some trouble with the Count last night. You should have run him out of town the first time he came back after Macgregor's murder.'

'The Count won't be hard to find when we want him. I'm more interested in the person here in town, who is our biggest worry.'

Grey looked down his nose for a second but then fixed Hewitt with a glare. 'You're still on that business that there's some criminal mastermind in Appsley behind all this,' he accused. 'Who is it this time? Is Dave Basset still suspected of robbing his own bank?'

'I'm not naming names and any rumours flying

about did not come from me. I feel, though, that I am worrying a few people and that's why someone tried to kill me last night.'

'It was the Count who tried to kill you last night.'

'He was not alone Two people were involved. The Count was in town on his own.'

'You don't know that for sure,' Grey said in a tone that defied contradiction. 'Those no-good Bramleys could have been hanging around and you might not have seen them.'

'I guess I'd better get back to work. I have the funny feeling that our killer friends might be planning another visit to Appsley.'

Grey never bothered to reply, just snorted in disbelief and began to examine the papers on his desk.

Hewitt's next stop was the Macgregors' store. He browsed around looking at the many items on display until Sue was finished with the lady she was serving.

With a welcoming smile, the girl walked over to where Hewitt was waiting. 'I heard that you had some trouble with the Count last night, Pete. Mother and I heard the shooting later in the night. It's nice to see that you are still in the one piece. The Count's very dangerous. Please be careful.'

'There's someone else around here a lot more dangerous than the Count. I fed a bit of information about and last night someone tried to kill me. I know that the Count will try to kill me one day too but the other one is much more dangerous. I think that person was also responsible for the murder of your father.'

'Do you know why?'

'I think I do but at this stage I can't say for sure. But be sure not to mention anything about those cartridges. If you do, you could put both your mother and yourself in great danger.'

Mullane was tired. He had ridden forty miles and was overdue for some sleep but felt it best to acquaint his men with the latest developments before turning in. Freeman and Turner were eager for news. Their current roles as hard-working cattlemen kept them away from notice but after a few weeks out on the range, even dull towns like Appsley attracted them.

'How were things in the big city?' Turner greeted as Mullane joined them for breakfast.

Freeman asked eagerly, 'Did you hear about our next job?'

'It will be soon. There's another shipment of money coming soon.'

Turner delayed the attack on his bacon and eggs. 'We won't get away with the same trick again, Clint. I reckon we should hit the coach on the road this time.'

A knowing smile flitted across Mullane's weather-beaten face. 'We won't be hitting any coaches. There's an easier way. We hit the bank while the money is stored overnight in the safe.'

'None of us knows how to blow a safe,' Freeman said in dismay. 'We would probably blow ourselves up if we tried it.'

'I know how to do it,' Mullane said. 'I saw it done once in Missouri. It's just a case of packing the charge right so that the force of the explosion is concentrated on the weakest place. The safe in the Appsley bank isn't very good quality. It's only made to keep honest people out.'

'And what is the bank messenger going to be doing while all this is going on?' Turner asked. He too had his doubts.

'He'll be sleeping like a baby in his bedroom quite convinced that the money is safely locked away.'

Freeman still was not convinced. 'What about that nosy lawman?'

'We had a half-hearted try at him last night. It didn't work but there's no harm done. The Count of No Account will get the blame and that will attract all of Hewitt's attention. He's starting to find out a few things so we might have to give him a lead pill eventually but not before we blow that safe.'

'What if he gets too nosy and comes out here?'

'That's different. Out here we can just make him disappear and our man in town can put about the story that he was scared off by the Count.'

Freeman, deep in thought, tugged at the end of his moustache. 'Folks are still likely to get curious. What if he tells someone that he's coming out here to see us?'

'You worry too much, Willie. There are plenty of places out here to hide a body and we can just deny that he ever came here. Now I'm going to get some sleep. You two get out on the range and let our neighbours see you. We have to keep looking respectable.'

TWELVE

Hewitt was out early and this time he rode alone. He had explained to Sue that he would not be riding with her that morning and actually left town before daylight. Two hours later he had crossed the eastern hills and was following Prospector's Creek.

Cattle had been watering along the creek and he saw a few different brands when he encountered them moving back to their feeding. A raw-boned, longhorned cow caught his attention as she trotted across his path. Her brand was Mullane's TG but the calf trotting at her side was freshly branded with back-to-back Bs, which he suspected would be the Bramleys' brand. 'Looks like the Bramley boys are adding rustling to their string of misdeeds,' he said to Cactus. 'Rustling like this is not even smart. Mullane's hands will soon see this calf.'

After the first calf Hewitt started paying attention to the cattle and soon discovered a couple more young steers wearing the wrong brand. These brands were a little older. He was puzzled. Such blatant rustling was stupid but if the TG riders had been doing their jobs someone would have spotted it and laid a complaint. He could only conclude that Mullane and his crew were not taking much interest in the welfare of their stock.

Freeman and Turner were riding aimlessly about seeking a shady spot where they could let their horses graze while they rested in the shade. Neither was very interested in the cattle and the spread was only lightly stocked. The ranch provided a façade of respectability and was never intended to be a great moneymaker.

They were riding around a hillside when they saw a string of cattle trotting past on a well-worn path below them that ran beside the creek. The animals came in single file led by a big spotted longhorn. Turner pointed at the cattle. 'Something's disturbed them. Cattle coming back from water usually don't trot like that.'

'Could be the Bramleys,' Freeman said. 'That pair of dumb jackasses think they're being smart by rustling a few calves but all they're doing is attracting attention to themselves. If the law ever comes sniffing around Prospector's Creek, who will they look at first, respectable ranchers or proven rustlers? Clint was smart to let them get away with a few calves. The law will never be able to rely on anything they might say about us.'

Movement on the valley floor suddenly caught

Turner's eye. 'Quick – get your horse in here among the trees,' he whispered urgently. 'Look who's just come round the bend in the creek.'

Both men wasted no time concealing themselves. They dismounted quickly and peered back through the foliage at the distant rider.

'He's still a long way away. Are you sure it's Hewitt?' Freeman whispered although the approaching rider could not possibly have heard him.

'It's him. That red horse with the white blaze is easy to spot. I hope he didn't see us.'

'I don't think he did. He seemed to be looking at those cattle.'

'What do we do if he has spotted us?' Turner was not quite so sure of the situation.

'It depends on the questions he asks. After all, this is open range. Our cattle are on it and we have every right to be here. We don't need to hide from the law.'

'Clint reckons he's finding out a bit too much. Maybe he's after us already. I think we should dry-gulch him here if we get the chance. Damnit, Willie, why didn't one of us bring a rifle?'

'Clint said not to,' Freeman reminded him. 'He wants us to look like law-abiding cowhands, not gunmen. But he sure wasn't thinking of a situation like this.'

'Do you think he has a rifle? If he has, he can drop the pair of us before we get into six-gun range.'

'I can't see one, unless he's carrying it on the near

side of his horse.'

Both men studied their intended victim whose fast-walking horse was rapidly approaching them, but, on the course he had chosen, the lawman would pass their position out of revolver range.

Hewitt saw no reason to think that the patch of trees and bushes up the hill and to his right, was any different from similar patches he had passed that day. His mind was on the rustled calves he had seen but he remained sufficiently alert to see the rider on the grey pony who suddenly appeared around the end of a ridge ahead.

The newcomer saw Hewitt, checked his mount, wheeled it about and galloped out of sight.

Turner and Freeman saw the deputy suddenly urge his mount after the grey and its rider. 'He's getting away,' Freeman said in a tone that was a mixture of both alarm and relief. He had not liked the situation that had been developing.

Turner chuckled, 'That was Elmer Bramley. He rides that grey a lot. This is getting better by the minute. Let's follow them. Then if we get the chance, we can shoot Hewitt and let the Bramleys take the blame for it.'

The lawman had chosen Cactus because he was range-raised, sure-footed and confident. He would follow any animal he was sent after and he knew now that he had to catch the grey. The sorrel seemed unhindered by the uneven, rocky ground and was soon at top speed. He shot past the hidden watchers well out of revolver range.

When Hewitt sighted his quarry again the man on the grey was spurring his mount towards a pine thicket in the hope that he would lose his pursuer. It could also allow him, if he felt inclined, to double back and wait in ambush for the man behind him. But he need not have worried.

When the lawman reached the trees, he could hear small branches breaking as the rider ahead smashed his way through the densely growing timber. In such terrain hitting trees was inevitable but a good horse in the brush chose the easiest path and did not dive under low branches that could sweep the rider from its back. A rider with confidence in his mount did only minimal steering, leaving the selection of their path to the horse, with its faster reflexes.

Bramley had never been much of a rider in the brush and avoided it wherever possible. Consequently his horses were not familiar with the task that now confronted the grey. The horse and rider, though, had different opinions about the safest route. The horse might select one side of a tree but Bramley, at the last moment, would decide that the other side looked better. The grey would try to answer the reins but sometimes had little room to move. More than once it bumped a tree and sometimes the rider's knee or foot collided painfully with a tree trunk. Where it had the chance to avoid a collision, the horse momentarily stopped and lost ground to its pursuer every time it did so.

Hewitt, in a particularly rough piece of country, halted Cactus briefly so as to hear the direction that his quarry was taking through the brush. It was obvious that he was not intending to stop and try an ambush. During the brief pause to listen, the deputy heard the sound of other horses behind him. His first thought was that Bramley had led him into a trap. He's smarter than I thought, he said to himself. Looking around, he saw a large boulder amid a patch of tall pine saplings. Quietly, he turned the sorrel behind the rock and crouched over its neck. There he waited.

The wait was not a long one. Two riders came out of the trees. 'Where's that star-toting sonofabitch?' an angry voice said. Someone else was not enjoying a fast, bruising ride through the timber.

Just then they heard Bramley's horse smashing through the brush ahead. 'He's over there,' another voice said.

Hewitt peered over the boulder and saw two riders disappearing among the trees as they followed the rancher. He could not get much of a look at either horseman and consequently saw nothing familiar about them.

He waited a short while to give the others time to move a fair distance away, then quietly rode back the way he had come. If nothing else he had learned that Prospector's Creek was not a safe place to ride. He resolved that he would visit the area again but next time would bring along a rifle and would try from a different direction.

It was mid-afternoon when he returned to Appsley. As he rode along the street he saw Mary Macgregor frantically waving to him from the store's balcony. He rode over and called up, 'Howdy Mrs Macgregor. Is there any trouble?'

'Not yet, but there will be. The Count's back in town. Be careful.'

THIRTEEN

Wilcox was waiting by the stage depot door. In response to his urgent gestures, Hewitt rode over to him.

'Just thought you ought to know, Pete. The Count's in town.'

'I know that. Mrs Macgregor just told me. Do you know where he is at present?'

Wilcox pointed. 'That bay horse hitched in front of the saloon is his. So I expect that he's inside. How are you going to handle this?'

Hewitt dismounted before replying. 'I don't want to start anything in the saloon where there could be innocent bystanders and it's not much safer out here in the street where stray bullets can go anywhere. I have to get him outside somehow.'

'Do you think you can handle him?'

'I won't know till I try. There's no easy way out this time.'

'You're damn right there isn't.'

The statement was accompanied by the double click of a gun being cocked and the Count emerged from around the corner of the building. His right hand held a gun that was trained on the deputy. 'This time, Hewitt, I have you dead to rights. Don't make a move towards your gun.'

The deputy turned to face the little gunman, whose normally expressionless face was actually smiling. 'I guess you fooled me that time, Count,' he admitted.

'I sure did. Now move out there in the middle of the street. I want plenty of witnesses.'

Hewitt knew that the gunman would not want witnesses to a murder and was much relieved to know that he still had some sort of chance. 'Are you figuring on a duel, Count?'

'Something like that, but I'm warning you. If you make one false move I'll kill you without giving you a chance.'

When Hewitt reached the middle of the street, his captor ordered him to stop and turn around. Then he also moved to the road's centre, halting about ten paces from the lawman. Ostentatiously he uncocked his gun and returned it to its holster. He stood there feet planted, hands poised over his gun butts.

The deputy took one look and stepped backwards.

'Running away won't save you, Hewitt. Are you getting scared?'

Hewitt did not reply but took another couple of backward steps.

'Damn you, Stay where you are. If you run I'll shoot you in the back. We're finishing this business here and now.'

The deputy stepped back again but kept his eyes fixed on the Count. The latter was poised on the balls of his feet, body tense, ready for instant action. Once again Hewitt stepped backwards.

This time the Count wasted no breath. 'Draw,' he called and his hands flashed to his guns.

Onlookers saw little difference in the speed as both men drew but the Count was first to shoot. He missed and fired left-handed, then another miss. Hewitt's first shot was better aimed and it struck the gambler's left upper arm. The bullet's impact twisted his body sideways and the gun fell from his hand. Off balance, the gambler fired instinctively with little attempt to aim. He missed again.

Hewitt fired one more, carefully aimed shot. The Count was punched straight backwards and crashed to the ground. The gun fell from his hand. Running forward, the deputy called, 'Stay there. Don't try to get up.'

If the Count heard him, he gave no indication. He muttered something incomprehensible, made a gurgling noise and slumped back to the dusty street.

'Count – can you hear me?' There was urgency in Hewitt's voice. A vital question remained unanswered.

'He can't hear you now, Pete,' Wilcox said quietly.

The deputy looked around to see his friend with a

rifle in his hands. Wilcox saw the direction of his glance and gave a grim smile. 'This rifle was just insurance in case you lost the fight. That murdering little skunk was not going to live long enough to celebrate.'

Hewitt holstered his gun and to his surprise found that a bullet had passed through the holster. One of the Count's shots had not missed by much.

Onlookers gathered quickly, for many had been watching the drama from a safe distance. More than one expressed the opinion that their new lawman had performed a long overdue public service, but the deputy was in no mood to celebrate. Once he had arranged for the Count's body to be collected, he returned to the sheriff's office to write a report for the coroner while events were still fresh in his mind.

An hour later he was still there, crossing out mistakes, rearranging sentences and generally making little progress. His mind was still racing and it was hard to concentrate on his task.

He was looking for an excuse to do something more interesting when Wilcox appeared at the door with a bottle of whiskey in his hand. 'You've done enough work for today, Pete. It's time to celebrate.'

'There's nothing to celebrate, John. I'm not in the mood. I didn't want to kill the Count but he forced the issue.'

'Just as I thought,' Wilcox said with the satisfied air of one whose suspicions had been confirmed. 'You're worrying about nothing. The Count was a murdering little skunk and you did us a big favour by shooting him. I was not too sure how it would go at first. When you started backing away, I figured you were about to turn tail and run.'

'I felt like it but I was working to a plan,' the deputy explained. 'A very fast gunman is most dangerous at short ranges. He doesn't take time to aim and he doesn't have to be far off-centre for his shots to miss over a bit of distance. Every foot you move back increases his chances of missing you. The Count was ready to go and did not want to disturb his concentration by moving closer when I moved back. By the time he woke up to what I was doing, I was out of the range where he shot best. I was lucky.'

'Lucky or not, you did a good job. Sheriff Anderson used to keep a couple of glasses in his desk drawer. Get 'em out and get the dust out of them. If you don't feel like celebrating, you can start drinking to forget.'

'You seem to have thought of everything. I'll have one with you but I want to keep a clear head. There's still a lot of work to do around here.' As he spoke the deputy took a couple of glasses from the desk drawer. There were a couple of chips out of the rims but they looked reasonably clean.

Wilcox poured a generous amount into each glass and handed one to Hewitt. 'Here's to the end of our troubles,' he said.

The deputy took a sip at the raw whiskey and shuddered slightly as it burned its way down his throat. 'I still have the problem of the missing strongbox and a few murders to worry about.'

Wilcox tossed down his drink with an ease that indicated a considerable amount of practice. He paused to catch his breath and said, 'With the Count out of the way you have the Macgregor case solved and I reckon that if you bring in the two Bramleys they'll soon confess to their part in the raid here in town. That pair aren't smart enough to stay out of trouble. You can bet your boots they were in that robbery.'

'I'm not so sure. Now put the cork back in that bottle and save it for another day. Thanks for the drink. I have to see Mrs Macgregor now and don't want to go over there smelling like a distillery.'

Wilcox looked a little disappointed but corked the bottle and transferred it to the side pocket of his coat. 'Are you sure it's Mrs Macgregor you want to see?' he teased. 'You wouldn't be planning to go riding with a certain young lady tomorrow, would you?'

Hewitt shook his head. 'Much to my regret, I won't be able to. I intend taking a ride out to Prospector's Creek instead.'

With a laugh Wilcox said, 'I think you'll find that Sue Macgregor is more pleasant company than the Bramleys.'

Both women were in the store when Hewitt arrived. Sue was serving a customer but her mother greeted him. 'I'm glad to see that you came through your encounter unscathed, Mr Hewitt. My poor husband can rest in peace now that his killer is gone.'

Hewitt was tempted to tell her of his doubts but decided that it might be safer for all concerned if he did not. Instead he asked if any new information had come to light about the missing box of cartridges.

'I think you should be looking for them at the Bramley ranch,' Mary told him. 'Max Bramley, when he was alive, did a bit of bird hunting and my Angus got those cartridges in for him because he had a twenty-gauge gun. Max was a good man, not like those layabout sons of his.'

'How long has Max Bramley been dead?'

'At least eighteen months to two years.'

'So the cartridges were here before he died?'

A look of surprise suddenly crossed the woman's face. 'No – I remember now. Those shells came in after Max died. He never picked them up and his sons never kept his store account going. The only way a box could be missing would be if it was a cash sale. It's possible one of the sons could have bought the cartridges from Angus over the counter but he didn't mention it. Why are you worrying so much about a box of cartridges?'

Hewitt looked about. The other customer had left the shop. 'It is very important that you say nothing to anyone about this. You and Sue could be in great danger if you do. I think those cartridges were linked to the coach robbery here in Appsley.'

Sue joined them. 'You two are looking very

serious,' she remarked.

'Your mother and I were discussing those missing cartridges.'

'Are they important any more?' Sue asked. 'The Count is dead and the two Bramleys will probably admit something if you start questioning them. They're not the brightest.'

Hewitt had other ideas but at that stage did not want to say too much. 'I think that the person who organized the strongbox robbery is still here in town. He's the one I'm after. Someone in Appsley planned this whole thing but took none of the risks that the bandits did. Whoever that someone is knew the money transfer business pretty well. I'll have to be getting back to work now. There are still people I need to talk to. Unfortunately I won't be riding in the morning, Sue. I will be riding but it won't just be to exercise my horse and it will be a long day.'

'That's a pity. I was enjoying our morning rides.'

'Let's hope we get the chance for a few more before I get moved on. Apparently the town council is complaining about me and is going to formally request that I be replaced. Mayor Grey seems to be all for law and order as long as he lays down the law and the rest follow his orders. How did Sheriff Anderson handle him?'

'They weren't the closest of friends but Anderson was doing a good job and the town liked him.'

'Not the whole town,' Hewitt observed. 'I have to

go now. When I get back I'll see you about riding again, Sue.'

The deputy was not looking forward to his next task.

Grey was not happy to see him and was not impressed when Hewitt informed him of his plans for the following day. 'We're paying you to keep order here in Appsley, not going gallivanting all round the country. Short of arresting them, you won't learn much from the Bramleys. They'll be in town on the weekend, why not wait till then?'

'I have my reasons. I'll let you know what develops.'

'I hope you will. Now, if you will excuse me, I'm a busy man. Don't get yourself shot tomorrow.'

'I'll try hard not to.'

FOURTEEN

Willie Freeman crouched on the ridge and carefully trained the telescope on the town below. The morning sun was just high enough to bathe the buildings in its light. Carefully he moved the instrument around until the window came into view. The signal was there arranged on the sill, a white towel and a red undershirt. It was a prearranged warning. The white meant Hewitt and the red meant danger.

Freeman cursed. He had been looking forward to an easy day, but now that trouble was headed their way the men on the TG ranch would have much to do. He collapsed the telescope and hurried to the horse he had left ground-tied below the skyline. Once mounted he turned the animal's head back down the slope to the path that ran beside Prospector's Creek. Freeman did not know how much time they had but he knew from the signal that Hewitt was on his way.

At first the trail was rough and rocky and he had to restrict his mount's pace, but as soon as the ground became more even he spurred the horse into a gallop. The others would need to know as soon as possible.

Turner and Mullane were in the barn feeding horses when they heard their companion returning at the gallop. They hurried outside just as Freeman hauled a foam-flecked horse to a halt. 'He's on his way. Hewitt's coming. I saw the signal.'

'What was it?' Mullane demanded.

'It was red and white. That was one of the signals you agreed on the last time you were in town.'

'That's right. Looks like that sneaky sonofabitch is creeping back along the creek again. Willie, get your rifle. He's not giving us the slip this time. We'll head back there and give him a little surprise.'

'What about me?' Turner asked.

Mullane paused a second while loading the rifle he had taken from the wall. 'Get under cover and watch that he doesn't come by road this time. He might try a new trick.'

'Do I kill him if he comes?'

'Not unless you have to. We don't want any signs of trouble here. It's best if we take him over to Bramleys and kill him. Who's going to believe a couple of drunken rustlers if a dead lawman is found on their ranch?'

Hewitt had left Appsley well before daylight, riding

south for several miles before he saw the fork that he sought in the trail. A rutted wagon road came in from the left and wound around the southern end of the mountains that rose so steeply east of the town.

The sun was well up in the sky as he passed what he guessed was the Bramley ranch house. It was a sun-faded building set back in a stand of pines about a hundred yards from the trail. A creek that he took to be Prospector's Creek flowed past the front of the house. No smoke was coming from the chimney and the lawman guessed that the brothers might still be asleep. He had heard from people who should have known that the pair would drink late into the night and never rose early.

The TG ranch house caught him by surprise. A couple of miles past the Bramley spread the lawman rounded a bend in the trail and the house was directly in front of him about a quarter of a mile away. The trail led through open country and there was no cover that allowed him to approach unobserved by anyone who happened to be watching.

Again there was no chimney smoke but Hewitt knew that the building might not be empty. The house was a shingle-roofed log cabin with corrals nearby and a barn behind it. A few horses grazed in the fenced area that surrounded the buildings. He passed through the gate, fastened it behind him and rode up to the front of the house. Halting near the front door he called, 'Anyone home?'

Silence.

He called again and upon receiving no response, rode around the back of the building. Recent prints of hoofs and boots told him that there had been considerable movement around house and barn earlier in the day.

Suddenly a horse inside the barn whinnied as it caught the scent of the intruders. Ranch horses were not usually stabled in summer unless they were ill or were needed for some special purpose. Surrendering to his curiosity, Hewitt dismounted and entered the barn through one of the double doors that had been left open. Inside, he saw not one but three horses standing in stalls, munching away at mangers still partly filled with grain.

One glance at the massive shoulders and hindquarters confirmed that the animals were quarter horses. On closer examination he saw that they were superbly fit, with big blocks of muscle under their carefully groomed hides. Someone had been giving the animals the right combination of feed and exercise. One was a dark chestnut and the others were bays.

With rising excitement Hewitt remembered the coach driver's description of the bandits' horses. Here they were. Hewitt was sure of that. What else would he find if he looked around? He doubted that he would find the money or the missing strongbox that had contained it but, in the hope that he might uncover some other clue, he started to look about the barn. The usual items of harness and broken straps and buckles hung on nails on the wall. But then his eye caught something that he had scarcely noticed before because it did not look out of place. A well-used saddle was on a rail between a couple of empty stalls. Where was the man who used it? He hoped that it was only a spare saddle but it lacked the dust that accumulated on equipment left in barns. With growing unease he looked around but he was too late.

Turner appeared from behind a stack of baled hay. The gun in his hand was aimed straight at Hewitt. 'Move and you're dead.'

The lawman did as he was told. Try to talk your way out, his mind told him, so he said, 'Seems like someone was home after all. I'm Pete Hewitt, a deputy sheriff. Are you Clint Mullane?'

'No I'm not. I'm Art Turner, I work for Mullane. Now what were you doing snooping around here?'

'I came around to the barn to see if someone was here. I heard the horses inside and went in. You have some good horses here. Do you intend to race them?'

'Shut up. I have the gun so I ask the questions. What are you up to, Hewitt?'

The lawman thought quickly. 'I came out to see if Mullane wanted to lay a rustling complaint against the Bramleys. I've seen their brand on calves following your cows. You must have seen them yourself.'

Turner's weather-beaten face twisted in a mirthless smile. 'We'd be blind if we didn't. But that's not your real reason for being here, is it? Now I want you to unbuckle your gun belt with your left hand and step away from it. One wrong move will be your last.'

With no other option, Hewitt obeyed. He played for time. 'What makes you think I'm here for anything else?'

'We know you've been looking for the ones who grabbed that money in Appsley. We know every move you've been making. You thought you were being smart but we're smarter. You've gone about as far as you're gonna go, Hewitt. You won't be riding away from here.'

'Don't do anything rash, Turner. There are people who know that I was coming out here. If I don't get back to Appsley they'll come looking for me. It's harder than you think to hide a body.'

Turner laughed aloud. 'We won't be hiding any body. Folks will find your carcass on Bramleys' ranch. It will look like you tried to arrest them for rustling and they got you instead. What jury would believe that a couple of no-goods like the Bramleys were innocent?'

Hewitt knew that his captor was talking sense and had no doubt that he was soon to be murdered. If he hoped to escape at all his chances would be better before the other two bandits arrived on the scene. He took a chance.

Saying nothing, he flicked his gaze over Turner's

shoulder as though something was happening out of the latter's range of vision. Instinctively Turner glanced over his shoulder. It was only for a split second but the deputy threw himself at him. His left hand brushed the gun aside and it exploded with a roar as Turner accidentally pulled the trigger. At the same time Hewitt smashed a hard right to the man's face. The punch landed but Hewitt was off balance and it was not as powerful as it should have been. Turner reeled back but did not go down. The deputy followed him, keeping in close and feeling for the gun. His hand found the cylinder and he clamped his fingers round it, stopping it turning as he tried to deflect the barrel away from his body. Turner butted him in the nose. Tears filled his eyes, blurring his vision, but he clung desperately to his opponent and ground his heel into the other's instep.

Blood was flowing from Hewitt's nose and it spattered Turner as he snorted to get his breath. Both threw punches and elbows at each other and then the deputy caught his opponent's left hand in his teeth. He bit down hard and Turner roared with pain as he tore his hand free but not before the teeth had ripped deep gouges in the edge of his palm.

Both were panting with exertion as they struggled, fully aware that the one who controlled the gun would be the ultimate victor. It was a frantic, brutal contest with little time to consider options, just two bloodspattered men fighting by sheer instinct.

Suddenly Hewitt felt that Turner was weakening.

Summoning up all his strength, he smashed an elbow into the other's face and twisted violently the gun he was holding.

Turner reeled backwards, involuntarily letting go the gun. Hewitt jumped back from him and his right hand reached around for the butt of the captured gun.

Then all went black.

FIFTEEN

His head ached, it hurt to move and there were voices. For a second or two Hewitt lay still and events came back to him.

A voice said, 'He's stirring. I thought at first that I might have hit him too hard.'

The deputy recognized Turner's voice. 'You got here just in time, Clint. He managed to get my gun. I thought I was a goner.'

'You're lucky I came back to check on things. Let's get this *hombre* on his feet.' Mullane leaned down. 'Get up, Hewitt.'

The deputy heard but did not stir. He needed time to think and there would be none if his captors thought he was conscious. The more helpless he appeared, the more careless he hoped they would get.

A boot thudded into his ribs. 'I said, get up.'

He allowed a soft moan to escape his lips but otherwise showed no sign of being conscious. The boot came again and painful though the kick was, he was determined not to react to it.

'Looks like you cracked his skull, Clint. I don't think he'll ever wake up. By the look of him he's just about dead.'

'Just about ain't good enough. He has to be well and truly dead. Saddle up a couple of those quarter horses. We'll cart this coyote over the back of Bramleys and hide the body.'

'What about Hewitt's horse? It looks a real good one.'

'That's right, Art. It's too good and too many people have noticed it. We'll get rid of Hewitt the same way as we got rid of that empty strongbox. We buried the box under a dead cow. Nobody thinks to shift a rotten carcass to look for something underneath. This time we'll bury Hewitt and shoot his horse on top of the grave. Folks will find the horse but they won't be looking under it. I would like to hear the Bramleys explaining how they happen to have the deputy's dead horse on their ranch,'

Hewitt forced himself to lie still as, none too gently, Mullane searched his pockets. The latter gave a whistle of surprise when he found the brass base of the twenty-gauge shell. 'This skunk ain't as dumb as we thought. I think he's figured out how the guard's gun blew up. But that won't do him a lot of good now. When you're finished there, pass me that bit of rope and get Hewitt's horse from out the front.'

A few minutes later the deputy found his hands

tied before him and Turner returned with Cactus. He looked at their prisoner doubtfully and asked, 'Shouldn't you tie his hands behind him, Clint?'

'No. He'll be easier to carry this way. We hook his wrists over the saddle horn and he's less likely to fall off. He's too heavy to keep lifting back on to the horse.'

Hewitt felt the rough rope being fastened tightly around his wrists but still pretended to be unconscious. He could not see it but his face was covered in blood and with a bleeding gash in the back of his head, he appeared to be more badly injured than he was. He went limp as the two men heaved him into his own saddle and slipped his bound wrists over the horn. Cactus danced nervously sideways and he almost fell off. It took a great effort of will to remain limp and not to try to remain on board. But one of his captors caught him and pushed him back into place.

Turner mounted and took the reins of Hewitt's horse. Mullane picked up the deputy's hat and jammed it on his head. Instructing Turner to start on his way, he announced that he would clean up in the barn and remove all traces of what had occurred there. 'I'll bring a shovel and catch up with you in a couple of minutes,' he said.

Hewitt, his face partly shielded by his hat brim, cautiously opened one eye. Turner had his horse's reins and his mount was held short but was still too far away for him to reach the other rider. He knew that he had to make his escape attempt while there was only one man guarding him.

His chance came at the ranch's front gate. The hinge was sagging and the gate did not swing easily. Turner leaned down from his saddle and lifted the gate wide enough for the horses to pass through. Hewitt saw that his own reins were looped around his captor's saddle horn, so he could not pull them loose. As Turner's attention was on the gate, the deputy reached forward with his bound hands and undid the throat latch of his bridle. The gunman was still trying to avoid bumping his knee on the gate when Hewitt swung his bound hands and clubbed him from his saddle. Then he pushed the crown piece of his bridle over his mount's ears so that the bridle fell free.

Turner tumbled on to the gate as his late prisoner drove the spurs into Cactus and sent him bounding away.

A shout from Mullane announced that he had seen what happened but he was too far away to prevent it. Turner was yelling threats and curses too as he untangled himself from the gate and climbed back into his saddle. By this time Hewitt had gained a lead that had him out of revolver range.

As Turner wheeled his mount about to pursue, the animal stepped into Hewitt's bridle that was still swinging from the saddle horn. By the time he was free from the tangle, Mullane had reached him. 'He's getting away, Clint. We have to get after him.'

'He's got no chance. We're on a pair of racing quarter horses. He won't outrun them. Now, let's go.'

Without the guidance of a bridle, Cactus was running erratically. He did not know where he was supposed to be going but he knew that his rider wanted him to gallop. He stretched his neck and started flinging yards of dusty road behind him.

Hewitt glanced over his shoulder and saw the pursuing riders. On the comparatively clear trail they would soon overhaul him. He snatched off his hat and awkwardly, with his still-bound hands, held the hat over the horse's eye. In an effort to get full vision, the horse turned off the trail on to a stretch of sloping ground that led up to a low ridge. Each time the horse attempted to turn downhill, Hewitt placed the hat on that side so that it turned away again. He quickly switched to the other side as the horse turned too much in that direction. Losing ground at every turn, he kept the horse headed up the slope. Loose rocks rolled back and a couple of times Cactus stumbled but did not slacken his pace. Every time he deviated from his course, the hat was there to steer him straight again.

When they reached the crest Hewitt turned the horse along it. About a mile away he saw that the ground sloped down to Prospector's Creek. He urged his mount in that direction.

The pursuers had not gained as they had expected and Mullane tried a couple of long shots with his Colt. But they missed their target and his efforts

111

accidentally turned to the deputy's advantage.

Willie Freeman had been guarding the trail by the creek, but on hearing the distant shots he mounted his horse and galloped for the ranch on the assumption that he would be needed where there was shooting. Consequently, he galloped back out of the valley and did not see Hewitt as he came down the slope behind him.

The descent to the valley floor was steep. Riding down it with no real control over his horse would have terrified the lawman at any other time but he knew it was his only chance to escape. He could only hope that his mount's rough-country experience as a cow pony would get them safely to the bottom. Trying to ignore the pain of his battered body, he locked his bound hands around the saddle horn and clung there.

Turner and Mullane had both lost a little ground. Their horses were used to race tracks and fairgrounds and the need to lift their feet higher seriously hampered the long, low, galloping actions that gave them their speed. Mullane's mount had tripped twice but managed to stay on its feet though it seriously dented its rider's confidence in the process. Warned by his companion's experience, Turner was a little more cautious in his riding and he too fell back as a result.

'These horses can't handle the rough ground,' Mullane called. 'We're losing him '

Turner disagreed. 'When he gets down there on

the level trail we'll soon catch up with him. We only need to get down this ridge in one piece and these horses will get the chance they need. We can still get the sonofabitch.'

When Hewitt's horse reached the trail below, he found little trouble in turning it toward Appsley. Cactus had learned what the hat meant and now would stick to the narrow path that led to the town. However the rider had no real means of checking his speed and could only hope that the animal did not gallop himself to exhaustion before they reached safety.

Mullane and Turner were within a hundred yards of their quarry when their horses reached the level ground. Mullane called, 'We've got him now, Art. Go to work on that horse.'

With more level footing the quarter horses threw themselves into their top speed. With necks stretched, ears laid back and foam flying from their bits, the horses renewed their efforts. Hewitt was beginning to have doubts again. Cactus actually had more racing blood than either of the other horses but the short-term, explosive energy of the quarter horses could quickly bring them into dangerous pistol range. He glanced over his shoulder, the gap had narrowed. It took a great effort of will to sit still and not use the spurs but some energy had to be kept in reserve. With no reins, he could not control the pace and could only hope that his horse's staying power was greater than that of those pursuing them.

The next time he glanced back, he saw that the two riders had halved the distance between them. Not only that, but Mullane had drawn his gun, He could only hope that the effort to close the distance was taking more out of the gunman's horse than it was from his own.

The first shot sounded close behind and something whizzed past Hewitt's ear. He glanced back and saw that Turner's horse had dropped back but Mullane was now within thirty yards. The next shot missed but it was time to call for a last effort from his horse. A light touch of the spurs and Cactus accelerated away with that final burst that was characteristic of his thoroughbred sire. It would only last a couple of hundred yards. Would it be enough? A bullet kicked up red dirt in front of the horse. The deputy heard another shot but it also missed. He looked back again. Mullane was now much further back. His horse was exhausted. The combination of rough ground and staying power had beaten short-term speed.

'You can ease up now, Cactus. You've beaten them.'

As if it understood, the horse needed no restraining hand to slow its pace. The pursuers were just dots in the distance when the animal slowed to a trot. He was covered in foam and sweat was running off him in streams but given time to catch his breath, he still had a gallop left in him. When the horse slowed to a walk his rider was able to concentrate on the ropes binding his hands. Using his teeth he was able to work loose the knot and free his hands. A horse used to neck reining will obey a loose rope around its neck so Hewitt used the broken piece of lariat to restore a measure of control.

Fondly he patted the sweaty neck. 'Just get me to Appsley now, old fella, and you can have a rest.'

SIXTEEN

Sue had been uneasy all morning. She had a feeling that Hewitt was in some sort of trouble. When there were no customers in the store she went upstairs and looked for him. The back windows offered a clear view of the eastern ridge where they had seen the strange riders and from the front balcony she could see a fair distance down the road leading from town.

It was early afternoon when she looked up at the ridge and saw the distant figure of a horseman. As the rider descended the ridge, she could identify Cactus and heaved a sigh of relief. Then she saw something else. Sunlight was flashing on something bright on the crest of the ridge. Though she could not see the origin of the flashes it looked as though someone was signalling and there seemed to be an urgency about it. From where he was Hewitt would not have been able to see the signals but the girl felt that he should know about them. After calling on her mother to mind the store, Sue walked to a place where she would intercept the deputy as he came into town. As he came closer, she saw that Cactus was caked in dusty sweat and had no bridle. Hewitt was covered in dried blood and sagged weakly in the saddle. He wore no gun and the rifle scabbard on the horse's side was empty.

Upon seeing the girl, Hewitt steered his horse to where she was waiting.

'Pete, what happened to you?'

'I found the bandits who stole the strongbox. Unfortunately they also found me and I'm very lucky to be here.'

'Are you badly hurt?'

'I have a rotten headache and need to get some cuts cleaned up but that will have to wait. I need guns, a fresh horse, and a few good men to help me.'

'Do you think those men will follow you into town?'

'Not if they have any sense. They'll soon be high-tailing it for parts unknown unless we can stop them.'

'I thought they might be following you because someone was up on the ridge behind you, signalling with a mirror or something. I could see the flashes.'

'At least one thing has gone right today,' Hewitt said. 'Their man in town is still here. I have to see Grey as soon as possible. I wonder if you would take Cactus down to the corral behind the office and unsaddle him for me.'

Sue looked concerned. 'I will, but you really should see about those cuts. You're gasping for breath too. You look awful.'

He handed her the ends of the rope he had looped around the horse's neck. 'I will get fixed up later but time's important at present.'

Grey was far from happy when the deputy acquainted him with what had occurred. He glared across his desk, his face flushed with anger. 'Why did you go out to Prospector's Creek on your own? You only succeeded in alerting those murderers. They'll run now and will be over the state line and headed for Mexico before we can even raise a posse. I can't believe that a lawman could be so irresponsible.'

Hewitt was in no mood for lectures even though he agreed with much of what the mayor had said. He replied angrily, 'I don't need you to tell me that I made a mistake. But I didn't know that I'd be walking into a trap. Someone in town here let them know that I was coming. One member of the gang is here in town.'

'Don't talk rubbish, Hewitt,' the mayor snapped. 'I've heard the story too about Dave Basset conspiring to rob his own bank and I don't believe it.'

'Neither do I,' the deputy said impatiently, 'but right now I'm more interested in those three men from the TG ranch. You did the legal work for the purchase of the ranch. What can you tell me about them?'

'I only dealt with Clint Mullane who bought the place. I know nothing about the others. They were just hired hands as far as I know. Dave Basset arranged the mortgage on the ranch. He might know who the others are but I doubt it. What do you intend doing now?'

Hewitt turned toward the door. 'I intend to telegraph Mullane's description to the law officers in the surrounding towns. Then I'll try to get a horse from somewhere and get a posse together. Will the town bear the cost of a hired horse for me and a dollar a day for each posse member?'

With an air of resignation, Grey shrugged his shoulders and said, 'I suppose so, but the council will expect to see some result for our money.'

'You'll get your result,' the lawman called angrily over his shoulder as he left the office.

The sun did not improve Hewitt's headache or temper as he walked out into the street. He was starting to ache all over as his other injuries cooled. It hurt to take a deep breath and he rightly concluded that he had at least one broken rib. The number of urgent tasks that confronted him seemed almost too much but they had to be done and he forced himself into action.

First he needed guns. The Count's guns were still in his office. He had been keeping them and a few other effects in case some relatives wished to claim them later. He hurried back there and took the guns from a locked closet. He strapped the cartridge belt around his waist and was reloading the weapons when Doctor Robson walked through the door. He looked concerned when he saw the deputy. 'Sue Macgregor said that you needed me. I can see that she was not being an alarmist.' He opened the bag he was carrying. 'Sit down there, young fellow, and let me have a good look at you.'

'There's no time now, Doc. I have to catch up with certain people.'

'You won't do that if you fall off the horse somewhere because of untreated head injuries. I'll be as quick as I can, so sit down here and don't argue.'

Sue was on her way to the sheriff's office when she saw John Wilcox fastening saddle-bags on a horse.

'Are you going somewhere, John?' she asked.

'I reckon so, Sue. Pete will be getting a posse together and I'll need to be ready to ride. I might take a quick ride around and see if I can get a few good men rounded up for him.'

'I'm not sure he'll be ready to ride for a while. Doctor Robson's patching him up now but he told me that he knows all about the raid on the town now and who's behind it.'

'Has he started naming names? I want to be sure that I don't tip off the wrong man while I'm rounding up some friends.'

'I haven't had time to ask him yet. He's been too busy rushing around but there's no reason to keep any secrets if he has the evidence he needs.'

'Sounds like Pete's getting somewhere at last,' Wilcox told her as he swung into the saddle. 'It could take me half an hour to get the men we need. Tell him I'll see him soon.'

Justin Bramley had just roped a TG calf and was tying it down to brand when he saw three riders appear on the crest of the hill that separated their ranch from the TG. He had almost been caught in the act and immediately concluded that he was deep in trouble.

He cast off his rope, abandoned it and vaulted into the saddle. As he raked his mount with the spurs he could see the three horsemen moving at a hard gallop. They were after him. A guilty conscience and his morning jolt of lunatic soup had assured him of that.

Elmer Bramley should have been with his brother but had been delayed when he found that his horse had thrown a shoe. He was in a corral about to rectify the problem as soon as his hands stopped their alcohol-induced shaking when he saw his brother riding hard towards him. Immediately he knew that something was wrong. He put down the horse's foot and ran for the Winchester rifle he always kept loaded and close at hand.

Justin hauled his lathered horse to a stop and jumped from the saddle. 'Mullane and the others – they're after me – caught me with one of their calves. They know we've been rustling their stock.'

Elmer cranked a round into his rifle's firing chamber. 'Grab your rifle. They ain't hangin' us as rustlers. There's only three of 'em.'

Mullane and his men could not have cared less about the Bramleys or the cattle that had only been a front for their operations. Veterans of the outlaw trail, they knew it was time to run. Hewitt's escape had destroyed their plans for a future raid on the Appsley bank. Their safe hideout was gone and soon the law would be on their trail. They saw Justin Bramley fleeing ahead of them but the small-time rustler had no part in their plans. Unfortunately the road passed in rifle range of the brothers' ranch house where both men, fuelled by alcoholic indignation, were waiting. They rode into a sudden hail of fire when they drew level with the front gate. The Bramleys were pouring in the lead as quickly as they could work their rifles. Not all their fire was accurate but the sheer volume meant that someone would be hit.

A bullet struck Turner's mount behind the girth, causing the animal to grunt and stagger sideways under the impact. Another took the hat from Mullane's head.

'It's an ambush,' he shouted, believing that he was dealing with a posse. 'Try to ride through.'

Freeman would have complied but a rifle bullet hit him under the left arm and ploughed into his heart. He slipped sideways and fell between his mount and Mullane's. One glance at the limp way the stricken man fell was sufficient to see that he was beyond help.

'Willie's gone,' Turner called. 'Keep riding.'

He was preaching to the converted because Mullane had no intention of stopping. It was every man for himself. He drove in his spurs and crouched low in the saddle as bullets flew around them.

'They're runnin'.' Justin laughed.

Elmer lowered his just-emptied rifle. 'They sure are. They ain't as tough as they thought they was.'

Justin looked after the retreating horsemen, now seen only as a small cloud of dust in the distance. The frown on his homely face did nothing to enhance his appearance. 'Something's wrong. They ran the wrong way. They should have turned around and headed for home.'

Elmer laughed as he reloaded his rifle. 'Who cares? They was too scared to worry about which way to go. Let's go and see that one we plugged. He might have money on him.'

SEVENTEEN

Hewitt had washed and changed into a clean shirt but was feeling only marginally better when he took a rather battered rifle from the wall rack in the office, loaded it and walked outside. The first person he met was Sue.

'You look a bit more presentable now,' the girl said with a smile.

'I wish I felt it. Have you seen John Wilcox about?'

'Yes. He's rounding up a posse for you.'

'Pigs' – the deputy remembered that he was in the presence of a lady – 'eyelashes he is. He's the gang's man in town. Where did you last see him?'

'He was on a horse. He rode down that side street over there just a minute ago. Are you sure he is involved?'

'I'm sure. I'm almost certain that he shot your father too.'

'But why? There was no reason.'

As Sue was speaking they saw a horseman emerge

from another street several blocks away. He lashed his mount with the rein ends and galloped out of town.

'There he goes,' Sue said as she pointed.

Hewitt left her in the middle of the street and sprinted to Cullinane's livery stable. A middle-aged half-breed who had been cleaning out stalls looked up in alarm as he ran into the stable.

'I'm the sheriff. Give me the best horse you have. Quick.'

'Bob mightn't like it, Sheriff.'

'That's too bad. There's a killer getting away. Don't waste time.'

The half-breed shambled down the row of stalls and led out a raw-boned bay horse. 'Most of the horses here are just livery plugs or town folks' ponies but old General here is the best of them. If it's serious business you'd better take him.'

'Thanks, I will but I'll have to ask you to toss a saddle on him. I think I might have a busted rib or two. I'm not sure I could lift a saddle on to him the way I am at present.'

The half-breed looked worried. 'Are you sure you're well enough to ride? Bob won't be happy if you fall off him somewhere and he loses the horse.'

'Right now, Bob's feelings aren't too important. Just get a saddle on that horse. I don't intend falling off him.'

A short time later the deputy in a borrowed saddle was leaving the stables just as Sue arrived. She immediately voiced her concern.

'Pete, you shouldn't be going after that man on your own. He might be meeting the rest of the gang.'

'If I'm lucky I'll catch him before then. I want this man more than the others. I think he is the brains behind the raiders and he's also the man who killed your father.'

'I can't understand why John Wilcox needed to kill Pa. Why would he do that?'

'Your father sold him that box of twenty-gauge cartridges. They link Wilcox directly to the killings and the robbery.'

'What do those cartridges have to do with the raid here?'

'I'll explain later. I have to go now. While we talk Wilcox is increasing his lead on me. I'll see you later.'

'Don't go after him alone, Pete. Round up a couple of men first.'

'I'm a stranger around here, Sue. I wouldn't know who to ask.'

'I do. Wait for me.'

'Sorry, Sue. I can't delay any longer. I have to get after Wilcox. He's the one with all the answers to the raid here.'

Hewitt hauled his iron-jawed mount around and set off out of town at a gallop.

Her face reflecting her concern, Sue looked after the disappearing rider and then hurried into the stable.

*

Turner's wounded horse gave out after it had travelled about a mile. It slowed to a stop, sat on its hindquarters and flopped on to its side. The rider felt it going and jumped clear, swearing loudly as he did so.

Mullane halted and looked down at his companion. 'Leave your carbine and saddle-bags and jump up behind me. We need to get you another horse mighty quick, so you'd better take your bridle. Get moving. That posse could soon be on our heels.'

'Danged horse is lyin' on my Winchester anyway,' Turner growled. 'But I can get at the saddle-bag and get my money out.'

Mullane looked nervously down the road expecting to see a posse ride into view at any moment.

Turner removed a calico moneybag from his saddle-bag and stuffed it down his shirt. Then he removed the bridle from the dying horse, hung it on his shoulder and sprung on to the rump of Mullane's horse. 'This horse ain't gonna get far with the two of us,' he growled.

'It only has to get us to Castle Butte. That's where Wilcox will meet us if he managed to get away. Then we can see about getting you another horse from one of the ranches.'

'Do you think Wilcox got away?'

'He probably did. We agreed that if we flashed that warning signal from the ridge he would know things had gone wrong and would get out of town pronto.

Ain't no one can accuse Johnny of being dumb.'

Turner felt far from being reassured. 'Ain't you forgettin' that posse that's most likely on our heels by now?'

'They're taking a long time to get after us. We should have heard their horses on the road by now.'

'I don't mind if they take their time,' Turner said as Mullane urged the horse to greater speed.

Hewitt was not enjoying the ride. General had spent much of his life in harness. He was rough-gaited and laid on the bit balancing himself against the rider's hands. A fit man would not have enjoyed the ride, and for one injured like the deputy it was an ordeal.

The tracks of Wilcox's galloping horse cut deeply into the hard clay road, making a fresh trail that was easy to follow and although uncomfortable, the bay horse lumbered along at a steady rate. As the miles rolled behind them, Hewitt began to realize that General had earned his reputation as a horse that could take hard work.

The trail rounded the end of a mountain spur. To the deputy's left lay a broad expanse of flat ground dotted with clumps of mesquite and cactus. Far across the plain a couple of flat-topped, low buttes appeared on the horizon. A tiny dust cloud showed where a rider was heading for the central butte. Any doubts as to the rider's identity were quickly dispelled when Hewitt saw where Wilcox had turned his horse off the trail. He followed.

Despite his rough gait, General had proved to have a reasonable turn of speed and plenty of endurance. The deputy knew that he would have made up ground on his quarry.

Aware that a dust cloud would be plainly visible for miles, Hewitt slowed his horse to a walk so that he would not betray his presence. Experience had taught him that fugitives rarely left the quickest means of escape unless it was to hide or to meet someone else. He did not stay on the tracks but moved from one clump of cover to the next. To ride the most direct way in plain view would be to invite an ambush. He had a hunch that because of its distinctive shape, the butte would be an ideal rendezvous place. It also offered a good vantage point for anyone who might be watching Wilcox's approach.

Once again, the deputy knew that he might have inadvertently ranged himself against superior odds. But this time he was determined that he would locate all his enemies before they discovered him.

Wilcox reined in when he reached the shadow of the butte. The day was hot and he was dry, having left town quickly when warned by the signal that plans had gone wrong and the law was on his trail. He rode about looking for any small creek or waterhole but saw none. At last, hoping that Mullane and his men might have a water canteen with them, he dismounted in the shade of an overhanging rock. Previously he had looked back over his trail but saw

no evidence that he was being followed. He hoped
that the wait would be a short one.

As soon as they saw there was no pursuit, Mullane
and Turner slowed their flight. To spare the horse
they took turns at walking and riding. Occasionally
both walked and led the animal. They had to
conserve its energy as much as possible.

Turner, as he had done many times, looked back
over his shoulder as he trudged beside the horse.
'Something's wrong. That posse that killed Willie
should be on our trail by now. Where are they?'

Mullane wiped a shirtsleeve over a sweaty
forehead. 'Maybe they found the money Willie was
carrying and split it up between them. Being rich
men they might have decided that risking lead
poisoning was no longer a good idea.'

'You don't reckon it was the Bramleys takin' shots
at us?'

'No. It sounded like a whole army was shooting at
us. There was lead flying everywhere. That pair of
drunks couldn't hit anything.'

Turner was still doubtful. 'A couple of Winchesters
can throw an awful lot of lead in a hurry.'

Any further argument ceased when Mullane
suddenly pointed ahead. 'There's the three buttes
over there. If he got clear of town, Wilcox will be
waiting there for us at the bottom of that centre one.'

'I hope he brought a spare horse,' Turner
muttered. 'I'm mighty sick of all this walkin'.'

'I doubt that he has but he might know the closest place where we can steal one.'

'What do we do if he ain't there?'

Mullane looked worried. 'We'll have to wait and see. We should know in another half-hour or so.'

EIGHTEEN

Wilcox had secured his horse in the mesquite and climbed to a large rock that gave him a good view over the green-dotted, red landscape. He looked first to the north-west, the direction from which a posse would come. He saw nothing. His gaze travelled in an arc until in the end he was looking north-east towards Prospector's Creek. A tiny, dark speck was moving down a stony ridge. He knew it was a horseman but he was expecting three. Where were the others? Anxiously he watched and then discerned that two men were approaching, one riding and the other on foot hidden behind his companion.

Hewitt's approach went unnoticed and, as he neared the tower of red rock, he was forced to stay in the brush and low-lying gullies. Consequently, he could not get a clear view of where Wilcox was waiting, if indeed he was there at all. If his man had not stopped at the buttes, Hewitt was merely wasting

132

time and extending the gap between them. A couple of hundred yards short of his goal, the deputy dismounted, hitched the horse in some sheltering brush and, rifle in hand, crept forward cautiously. From his position, he could see nothing of the men approaching from the other direction.

Wilcox soon recognized Mullane's red shirt that he habitually wore. Standing on top of the rock, he waved his hat to attract attention. His gesture worked and he saw the newcomers turn in his direction.

Hewitt was surprised to see Wilcox standing in plain view on the rock, then he saw that he was signalling to someone. The stage company man was not alone. Again the deputy had the feeling that he might have bitten off more than he could chew. With growing anxiety he stole forward, crouched low and took advantage of every bit of cover that was available. Bent as he was the broken rib was painful, but it was preferable to being hit by a bullet. He was nearing the base of the rock when he heard a horse approaching from his left and a murmur of voices.

Cautiously he peered around the edge of a boulder. About fifty yards away Wilcox was standing in the open, looking away from him. Then Mullane and Turner came into view.

'Where's Willie?' Wilcox's voice carried clearly in the hot, still air.

Mullane replied, 'A posse was waiting for us at Bramleys' and opened fire as we passed. They got Willie and Art's horse.'

'Couldn't have been a posse,' Wilcox declared in disbelief. 'I came straight from Appsley. Hewitt had just arrived. He had no time to organize a posse. He looked pretty beaten up so it could be a while before he gets on our trail.'

'Well, someone sure shot at us,' Turner growled. 'Willie wasn't killed by no imaginary bullets and that horse of mine didn't die of old age.'

'If it wasn't a posse, it must have been those no-good Bramleys,' Mullane muttered. Then he said ominously. 'When all this is over I'm coming back to let daylight through that pair of skunks.'

Wilcox brought him back to the situation in hand. 'Forget them. We need another horse and we need it fast. Do you know where we're most likely to pick one up?'

Mullane pointed to the east. 'Ferguson's ranch is a few miles that way. Maybe we can get one there.'

Turner was not too enthusiastic about that prospect as he was sure that it would involve a long walk for him.

Mullane hitched his horse beside that of Wilcox to a branch of a stunted cedar that afforded a small degree of shade. 'Let's get out of the sun,' he said, 'and figure out our next move.'

'Don't take too long. There could be a posse on the way,' Wilcox warned.

'My horse needs a rest. We can see for miles from here. If a posse comes after us they can't help raising dust and we should see that easily enough.'

Hewitt edged closer. He could see where the horses were tied. If he could cut the others off from their mounts the chance existed that they would surrender. He thought it unlikely but did not relish the thought of killing men without giving them an option to save their lives. After all, he had a rifle and could keep out of six-gun range, so the odds were not as daunting as they had first appeared. The distance between them was nothing to a man with a rifle but too great for accurate revolver work.

The three were deep in conversation, sitting on their haunches in the shade, when the deputy made his move.

'Get your hands up!'

Rather than comply, the trio scattered grabbing for their guns as they scurried for cover.

Hewitt fired at Turner who was slower to reach the sheltering rocks than his companions. The bullet whined off a boulder a good yard from its target. To make matters worse the next cartridge did not feed smoothly and it was necessary to jiggle the lever slightly before it slipped into the firing chamber.

Mullane sprinted for the horses. Hewitt was unsure whether he was trying to escape or attempting to get a rifle from his saddle, but he snapped a shot in his direction. Again the bullet went wide but this time luck was on the deputy's side. The slug clipped a small branch from the tree where the horses were tethered. The animals jerked back in fright, one breaking its bridle and the other snapping off the thin branch to which it was tied. Both wheeled about and fled.

Mullane was temporarily exposed but the deputy was still having trouble reloading his rifle. The big gunman had time to dive behind a rock before the lawman could bring his weapon into play again.

Wilcox and Turner had taken cover and now began firing back at Hewitt whose position gun smoke had betrayed. If lacking in accuracy because of the short barrels, the revolvers still had the range and killing power needed to account for their attacker.

Hewitt was cursing as a couple of bullets whined past him. The rifle refused to feed from the magazine and by then he was convinced that the sights were also out of alignment. He had assumed that the weapon was serviceable when he took it from the sheriff's office wall. It was far from comforting to find out that his assumption had been wrong. The weapon could still be used for single shots but with the sights the way they were it would simply be a waste of ammunition.

The odds had tipped back in favour of his enemies. Once more Hewitt had bitten off more than he could chew.

NINETEEN

Mullane and the others had seen their share of gunfights and after the first frantic rush for cover had settled down to take stock of the situation. They had the advantage of numbers and the added incentive was that if they could kill Hewitt and capture his horse, they could soon round up the runaways.

'He's on his own,' Willcox shouted. 'Spread out. He can't shoot three ways at once.' Then he called to the deputy. 'You don't have to get killed, Pete. Leave your horse and your rifle and you can walk away.'

'You know I can't do that,' Hewitt called back. 'And I wouldn't trust you murdering skunks either. You'll have to get past me to get that horse.'

'That's your last chance,' Mullane yelled.

The lawman wasted no breath in replying. The rifle that should have tipped the balance in his favour was virtually useless. He should have checked it before leaving Appsley. But now was no time for self-reproach. He knew that there was sufficient cover for his enemies to begin flanking his position and had to work out the best way to prevent such attacks.

The rifle gave him an idea. He loaded it, pushed the muzzle through a narrow space between two rocks and fired a shot in Wilcox's general direction. The movement and powder smoke gave the position away but that was intentional. He propped the rifle on some stones, aware that his enemies could just see the tip of the barrel. Then, belly down, painfully propelling himself with knees and elbows, he kept below the low mesquite and crawled back to a dry wash where he found better concealment behind a thick clump of cactus and was closer to where he had hidden his horse. There, peering through the spiky plants that grew on the lip of the shallow gully, he settled down to wait.

A gun fired and he heard the bullet ricochet from the rocks where he had left the rifle. One of the gang had tried a long shot, hoping that a lucky bullet might slip between the rocks and kill the rifleman he supposed was there. Hewitt smiled to himself. At least that part of the plan had worked.

Reason was telling the deputy that he would have a good chance if he retreated to his horse and galloped away but some sort of stubborn pride kept him where he was. He had done all the running he intended to do. He could not risk the Appsley raiders escaping again.

Mullane had been working his way from one piece of cover to the next moving in a wide arc that he hoped would bring him in on the lawman's left. He was a good hunter and moved as silently as possible while keeping low to the ground. The cluster of red boulders from which Hewitt had fired was about a hundred yards away. Wilcox had thrown the odd shot in its direction to keep Hewitt from sighting the two flankers but no shots had come back.

The big gunman was hoping that a bullet might have found its way between the rocks and already accounted for the lawman. But he was too much of a realist to bank on it. He would take his time and stalk the position carefully.

Hewitt knew from the way that Wilcox was wasting lead on his old position that the shooting was merely a diversion. He was sure that Mullane and Turner were working wide of him. He had to see them before they saw him. But where were they? Was one or both of them already behind him? Aware that movement might attract attention, he swivelled his eyes from side to side hoping to see the approaching danger. He tried to estimate how long it had been since the shooting started and then tried to figure the distance that a man could creep in that time; but then, he had no idea of the time involved. The mental calculations were distracting too. His best defence, he decided, was to remain alert and see the danger first.

His first warning was a splash of red showing

briefly through a small gap in the mesquite. He knew it was Mullane's red shirt but where was Turner? If he turned his head to look to the other side, he was sure that one or both of the raiders would detect the movement. He could only hope that Turner had not already seen him.

Mullane crept closer and Hewitt cocked his gun so that the sound would not betray him later. He concentrated on the shrubbery. Mesquite does not have thick foliage and he soon picked up his man again. He was closer now but still too far for accurate pistol shooting.

Wilcox had stopped shooting. For all the lawman knew, he too might have been stealing towards him, having discovered his deception. He was thankful that the large clump of cactus offered better concealment for him than the mesquite through which his enemies would have to approach.

When he glimpsed movement again Hewitt was amazed at how close Mullane had managed to get without being seen. He was barely twenty yards away but was looking in the wrong direction. The raider was still stalking the lawman's first position in the red boulders.

Hewitt no longer felt obliged to issue any warning. He sighted on the unsuspecting raider and squeezed the trigger.

At that moment Mullane moved slightly and the bullet that should have knocked him out of the fight merely burned across the back of his left shoulder.

His reaction was swift.

A bullet tore through a fleshy cactus splashing juice on its intended target who was barely inches from it. But Hewitt had the bigger target. His next shot tore through Mullane's upper arm, smashing it. The gun fell from Mullane's hand but in desperation he snatched it up with his left hand and turned once more to face his attacker. This action presented the deputy with a bigger target and he did not miss. He saw the gun fly from the raider's hand as a bullet ploughed into his chest. Satisfied that one opponent was out of the fight, Hewitt looked for the others.

Turner was not hard to find. He came charging in from the right dodging around obstacles and jumping others in his rush to get into effective range while Hewitt was distracted. The long-barrelled Smith & Wesson in his hand spat lead as he ran. Fortunately for the lawman, a running man does not shoot a revolver very well. One slug kicked up dirt a foot or so from where Hewitt crouched but the two that followed went wide.

By contrast, the deputy was shooting from a stable position and had no difficulty in sending a slug into the raider's midriff. Turner staggered as though he had hit an invisible wall, doubled over and fell. Though seriously wounded he had the presence of mind to fire another shot at his opponent before rolling behind a low rocky outcrop.

Hewitt took a chance and switched his attention back to where he could see Wilcox standing near the

141

boulders where he had left his rifle. The range was too great for accurate shooting but he fired the remaining cartridges at the man to ensure that he kept his distance. The shots had the desired effect and Wilcox disappeared behind cover. Leaving one fully loaded gun in easy reach, the lawman worked quickly to punch out the empty shells and fully reload the weapon he had just emptied. Much of the operation he did by feel because he had wounded enemies both within effective pistol range and he had to keep watching for signs that one or the other might resume the fight. He thought Mullane was dead but could not be sure. He was the type who would remain dangerous as long as he was conscious and able to pick up a gun.

He knew that he had reduced the odds against him but Hewitt was only too aware of how fortunes could change for the one who made a mistake.

TWENTY

'Clint,' Wilcox's voice floated across the comparatively open ground, 'can you see him?'

The effort of shouting would hurt but Hewitt could not resist calling back. 'I doubt that he's seeing anything, John. Surrender while you still can.'

'You don't sound too good yourself, Pete. I reckon you could be carrying a slug in you. Given enough time you might pass out and I can just walk over there and take that horse— Don't be a fool. Mullane and Turner are both carrying a lot of money. You don't have to tell anyone about it. Let me have that horse and you can claim that I got away with all the loot from the raid.'

'Forget it, John. I haven't been hit by any bullets and when it comes to gun fights I reckon I've had more practice than you. You haven—'

A gunshot interrupted Hewitt and a spray of dirt and stones stung his face as a bullet struck the bank in front of him. He twisted to see Turner on hands

143

and knees cocking his gun for a second shot. If the shooter had not been so badly wounded, the first shot would have killed the lawman. With a violently shaking hand, the raider raised his gun again. But Hewitt shot first. Turner's supporting arm collapsed and he fell forward on his face. This time he really was out of the fight.

By the time that Hewitt switched his gaze back toward Wilcox, the latter had fled the scene. He reappeared briefly from around some boulders, too far away to try a chance shot. Then he ran behind a couple more big rocks and the lawman lost sight of him.

He was stiff and sore and it took the deputy a while to get to his feet but this time he took no chances. Although Wilcox was increasing his lead, he took his time and checked to ensure that both Mullane and Turner were dead. He also collected their six-shooters and concealed them under some bushes. There was always the possibility that Wilcox might double back and seek to use the weapons against him.

Walking was not easy in his present state so Hewitt went to where he had left his horse. This time he would hunt his man on horseback and the extra height would enable him to see over some of the lower mesquite and cactus. That was the theory, but suddenly the everyday effort of mounting a horse seemed to be beyond him. He tried to lift his foot to the stirrup and found that he could not. Surprised by such weakness, he led the horse to a dry wash so that he could stand on the bank and mount from there. The horse was restless and moved about as he tried to get his foot into the stirrup but he eventually succeeded. It took all his strength to swing his right leg over the animal's rump and the sore side pained the lawman sharply as he settled into the saddle. It was then that he saw the other riders approaching.

There were three of them and the small figure on the black pony looked familiar even at a distance. He turned his horse towards the newcomers. Soon there was no doubt as to their identity. Sue was cantering towards him and Bob Cullinane and his half-breed stable hand were riding with her.

'Sue,' he called as the riders got closer. 'What in tarnation are you doing here?'

'I brought you a posse. You know Bob and Charley here used to scout for the army. He tracked you for us. You look awful. We passed a couple of loose horses back on the road. What's been happening?'

'Wilcox met a couple of the raiders here. They wouldn't surrender and I had to kill two of them. Wilcox has bolted into the rocks over there. He's on foot but he's armed. I want you to stay well out of this, Sue. Keep on your horse and wait over here.'

'Not so fast,' the girl said sternly. 'If I hadn't been keeping an eye on you, you could have been in a whole lot of trouble around about now. And I want a few answers. Before you left town in such a hurry, you told me that John Wilcox killed my father. I want to know why.'

'Wilcox turned the guard's shotgun into a bomb by placing a twenty-gauge cartridge in each barrel. They are just big enough to be caught at the end of the firing chamber and it is possible to load a twelve-gauge cartridge in behind them without seeing them in the gun. That's why twelve- and twenty-gauge cartridges should never be stored together. A man in a hurry can mistake a twenty for a twelve and someone else thinking the gun is empty can put another cartridge behind it. Wilcox was with me when I found the base of a twenty-gauge shell near the scene of the fight and guessed that I might start asking questions. I'm pretty sure he killed your father because he would remember selling him the cartridges needed to doctor the gun.'

'But if you knew this, why didn't you arrest him?' There was anger in the girl's tone.

'I wasn't sure who had bought those cartridges and was looking around for evidence. I didn't know for sure what had really happened until the raiders caught me for a while out at Prospector's Creek. I knew they were exchanging signals with someone in town but was not sure who until Wilcox panicked and ran.'

Cullinane was looking at the rocks ahead, hoping to see the fugitive, but he was listening. 'So you reckon Wilcox planned the raid as well?'

Hewitt nodded grimly. 'He not only planned it. I think he actually took part in it. From the side door of his office he could see into the street. I think he

146

might have shot the sheriff and the bank clerk. Men shooting from galloping horses don't shoot all that well and from what I can gather, they were shot from an odd angle. Witnesses all agreed there was so much shooting and commotion that another couple of shots would not have been noticed.'

Charley moved his wad of chewing tobacco to the other side of his jaw and spat. 'That murderin'—' Then he remembered Sue's presence and abruptly fell silent.

'Were you about to call him a murdering son of a bitch?' the girl asked. 'Because if you were, Charley, the description fits him exactly.'

Cullmane roared laughing but Charley looked shocked. He had never heard a respectable lady use such language.

'I worked a lot with Ross Anderson,' the half-breed muttered. 'He was a mighty good sheriff. It ain't right him getting bushwhacked like that.'

Cullinane brought them back to the present. 'Just how do you suggest we go after Wilcox?' he asked Hewitt.

The deputy looked about at the landscape, paused a while, then said, 'If you agree, Charley, we will get you to track him. Bob and I will keep an eye out for Wilcox. Don't go round any blind corners. If you come to one, I'll go round first. Then you can pick up the tracks again. We can leave the horses here with Sue.'

'You're not getting rid of me that easily. I can

147

shoot and I have brought a rifle along. I want to have a few words with John Wilcox.'

Hewitt did not approve and told her, 'Bob and I have to protect Charley while he is tracking and we can't do that properly if we are continually looking to see that you are not in danger. You are a real help holding the horses but are only a problem if you insist on going after Wilcox yourself.'

Sue did not like the situation but realized the sense of the lawman's words. 'All right, I'll stay here and keep out of the way,' she snapped angrily.

Wilcox had been close to despair when the other riders arrived. He recognized Charley's distinctive pinto pony from a fair distance away and knew that the half-breed could follow a track like a human hound. He could see that his pursuers were in no hurry. They did not need to be. He really had nowhere to go. At first he fled around the base of the butte but then he was confronted by miles of open country where it would be simple to track him. Outnumbered and on foot he would have no chance. Then he looked at the rock towering above him. If he could get above his hunters there might still be a chance of escape.

Stepping from one exposed section of rock to another, he found a fissure in the rocky wall that allowed him to begin his climb. At first there were plenty of handholds and footholds and the rock was not as steep as it had first appeared. About thirty feet up, he was surprised to find a ledge that ran around the corner of the butte. It was wide enough for him to crawl along without being visible from the ground.

Peering round the edge of a rock, he saw the posse some distance away on the flat ground. There were four horses guarded by one person and three men on foot were walking cautiously toward his place of sanctuary. There was no mistaking the bulky figure of Half-Breed Charley, slightly in advance of the other two. He knew that one of them was Hewitt and the other looked like Charley's boss, Bob Cullinane. None of the approaching trio was looking up at his hiding place.

His options were limited but Wilcox hoped that if he could kill the deputy, the others might be scared off sufficiently for him to descend and try to capture a horse. With Hewitt out of the way and the offer of wealth, the others might even be prepared to do a deal. The plan was optimistic, he knew, but short of surrendering he had no other chance.

His first task was to get rid of the lawman.

Charley was looking about and pointing out the scuff marks in the soft red earth. 'He's been here and he's been runnin' hard. He's one mighty scared *hombre* at present.'

Hewitt looked around. 'Be careful, Charlie. The scared ones can be unpredictable. Just take your time and don't take any risks. John Wilcox has killed too many good men already.'

'He's trying not to leave tracks,' Charley said. 'He's staying on the rocks but he'll step off somewhere and

149

I'll see where he does.'

'I reckon he's hiding around here somewhere,' Cullinane said as he looked about. 'Could be waiting to bushwhack us.'

The deputy agreed. 'I reckon he is. He sure as hell is not running.'

Charley pointed to a piece of broken, crumbling rock and boot scrapes leading up to a narrow, sloping ledge. 'He's gone up. He's like a bear in a tree. There's nowhere else to go. We've got him now.'

Hewitt looked up and cupped his hands around his mouth. 'Wilcox,' he shouted. 'Come down.'

The shout echoed back from the frowning red walls but there was no reply. The lawman looked upwards but saw nothing.

'There's no water up there,' Cullinane said. 'He'll have a mighty dry time of it. He left town in a hurry so I reckon it's been a while since he had a drink.'

Hewitt pushed back his hat and wiped a shirtsleeve over a sweaty forehead. 'It's too risky going up there after him. We'll just have to wait till he comes down.'

Charley had another idea. 'There could be another place somewhere around this butte where he can come down. Three of us can't surround this whole place. It's too big. It's best if we get our horses and spread out a bit. When we are a way off we should be able to see him if he moves around the rock. There's not many places where he can hide.'

'What if he waits for dark and then tries to sneak down again?' Cullinane asked.

The tracker shook his head. 'That place is bad enough to climb round in daytime. There's rotten rock everywhere. I figure he's learned that by now and won't dare try to escape in the dark. If he's got a lick of sense, he'll stay put once night falls. If we can keep him treed long enough, thirst will eventually drive him down.'

'I'll get the horses,' Hewitt volunteered. 'Then we can spread out and patrol around this butte keeping out of pistol range. We might even see where Wilcox is hiding.'

The deputy left the others and started walking around to the other side of the towering rocks. Much to his relief, Sue had followed orders and was waiting at a safe distance with the horses.

Thinking to save his aching body a bit of extra effort, the lawman stood on a rock and waved his hat to the girl as a signal to bring forward the horses.

Above him, concealed on a narrow ledge, Wilcox could not believe his luck. Hewitt was directly below him and totally unsuspecting. He leaned over the lip of the rocky shelf, cocked his revolver and sighted on the lawman below. Carefully his finger applied pressure to the trigger.

TWENTY-ONE

Hewitt was sure that Sue had gone crazy when he saw her suddenly snatch a rifle from the saddle scabbard on her pony and seemingly aim at him. He was jumping from his vantage point when he heard the rifle bullet whine off the face of the rock behind him. A shout of alarm, a clatter of falling rocks and a body crashing nearby added further to his state of confusion.

John Wilcox was sprawled on the ground a few paces away, face down and unmoving. Not far away lay a revolver, still cocked, that had survived the fall without discharging. Hewitt checked for signs of life but found none. The dead man's skull and the awkward angle of his head indicated that he had fallen head first on to the rocks below him.

Sue was approaching at the gallop, towing the other horses behind her. Cullinane and Charley had both sprinted back and all seemed to arrive simultaneously.

The girl flung herself from the saddle and ran to Hewitt. 'Pete, are you all right? I was frightened that Wilcox would shoot you before I could fire. I saw him just in time.' She glanced at the body and shuddered. 'I didn't want to kill him but I couldn't let him shoot you.'

Hewitt put an arm around her. 'You saved my life,' he said as he held her close. 'But you didn't kill him. The fall did that. Your shot missed him but must have scared him into making a wrong move and a bit of that ledge gave way. You can see there's some rock that came down with him.'

Cullinane smiled and told Sue, 'Looks like you saved us having to get a new lawman. That was good work.'

Hewitt said ruefully, 'You might need a new lawman. I must be getting careless.'

'That's the trouble with white men,' Charley joked. 'They never look up. You're lucky to have this little gal looking after you.'

'I know that. I wonder if she'd take on the job on a permanent basis.'

'Looks like it's all over with the Appsley raiders now,' Cullinane observed.

Hewitt shook his head 'There were four men involved. We have only accounted for three. There's another one to find.'

'So what happens now?' Sue asked.

'If you will look after the horses, the rest of us will search the bodies and get them all into one place.

Then, if you and Bob go back to town and arrange for a wagon to come out for the bodies, I'll try to talk Charley here into backtracking Turner and Mullane. I need to find what happened to the fourth man. If you see those loose horses on the way back to town, you could pick them up too. There might be something in the saddle-bags that is useful to this case.' Hewitt turned to Charley. 'Will you help me out with a bit of tracking?'

'Sure will. It beats working in that stable.'

Half an hour later their work at the buttes was finished. The three dead men were all carrying large amounts of cash. When totalled it came to nearly $6,000. Hewitt had no doubt that it was money taken in the Appsley raid. He was sore and felt incredibly weary but knew that he had another long ride before he could rest. He had to know what happened to the missing raider.

Sue was concerned about him and wanted him to return to town but he refused. He had to get on the trail while it was still hot.

They parted company then and Hewitt forced himself to ignore his pain and concentrate on the landscape that held the tracks.

Charley had no difficulty following the prints left by a mounted man and another on foot. An hour later they found Turner's dead horse. Noting that it had been shot, the lawman thought at first that there had been some disagreement among the gang. Charley thought the same and ventured the opinion that they might find the missing man dead on the trail.

They came over a rise and found themselves in sight of the Bramley ranch.

Charley chuckled and pointed. 'That's a sight you don't see very often; the Bramley boys are actually working.'

When they came closer, Hewitt saw that they had a pair of mules and were dragging a dead horse from the road in front of the ranch house. Both were so engrossed in their task that they failed to see the riders approaching.

Justin was handling the reins of the mules and glanced behind to ensure that his brother had fastened the chain properly around the dead horse. He saw the two horsemen and gave a croak of alarm.

'They're back,' he called and sprinted for the ranch house.

Hewitt kicked his horse into a gallop and drew a gun as he raced to head him off. 'Stay where you are, Bramley, or I'll shoot.'

For the first time in his life, Justin Bramley was pleased to see a law officer. A sideways glance showed his brother, hands high, menaced by Charley's gun. 'We didn't mean to shoot him,' the big man whined. 'They just came shooting at me and Elmer.'

'Who came shooting at you?'

'Mullane and the others. They just went crazy – came charging down the road shooting at us.'

'Did you shoot back?'

155

'Sure we did. We though it was them raiders that robbed the coach in Appsley.'

'For once, you could have been right. Now, where's the man who was riding this horse?'

'It was Willie Freeman.' Bramley pointed to a canvas-wrapped bundle some distance away under the shade of a pecan tree. 'We was getting him ready to take to town,' he lied.

Hewitt regarded him suspiciously. 'You wouldn't have been about to conceal the body so that no one knew he'd been here?'

Bramley tried hard to look the picture of innocence but, due to his unfamiliarity with that condition, he was hardly convincing. 'Now why would we want to do that?'

'Because he was carrying some of the money that was stolen in Appsley. Now don't mess me around, Justin. I'm not feeling well and I want to get back to town. You can co-operate now or get arrested and go to town with us. Make up your mind.'

'You can't arrest us. We never did anything wrong. Freeman and the others attacked us. It was self-defence. You said yourself they was bandits.'

'For all we know, you pair could have been in cahoots with Mullane and the others,' Hewitt reminded him.' It could have been a case of thieves falling out. Now, where's the money that Freeman was carrying?'

Justin still tried to maintain his bluff. 'Money – what money?'

The weary lawman's patience finally snapped. He raised his voice but even then it did not come out as strongly as he had hoped. 'Freeman was carrying part of the money taken at the Appsley raid. I intend searching your house and if I find any money there, you and your brother are going to be arrested for complicity in the robbery and murders. And if the bullet hole in the dear departed over there is not dead centre in front I'll charge you with his murder too. Now, are you sure you don't have any large sum of money?'

As though he had just remembered, Bramley said, 'Oh, *that* money. We was so busy here I plumb forgot about it.'

They found the cash on a table among the dirty dishes from the day's meals. It had been divided into two neat piles, the only things in the kitchen that were neat. While Charley watched the Bramleys, Hewitt counted the money. It came to just over $1,100.

The brothers looked like two small boys who had just had their Christmas presents snatched away from them, but then an expression like that of a coyote eyeing an unguarded chicken coop came to Elmer's face. 'Willie Freeman,' he asked Hewitt. 'Is he a wanted man?'

'I don't know. He might be. I'll have to make some more enquiries about his background.'

'If there's a reward out for him, me and Justin are claiming it.'

'Before you can be considered you need to give all the help you can in closing this business. At this stage I'm not interested in some calves trotting about with strange brands on them but if you are careful what you brand in future and tell all you know about your neighbours, I promise I'll support any claim you make for a possible reward on Freeman. Remember though, those TG cattle belong to someone and if I see any wrong brands on calves after today, you pair will be in big trouble.'

Two days later Hewitt attended a meeting of the town council. Basset and Grey were there wearing their usual looks of disapproval. Three other businessmen made up the rest of the group.

The meeting opened with the mayor grudgingly congratulating the lawman on closing the chapter on the Appsley raid. He was secretly disappointed with a situation where it was not possible for him to claim any credit but he was determined to put a good face on things.

Basset was not so gracious. 'Where's the rest of the money?' he asked with a strong note of accusation in his voice.

'Probably spent,' Hewitt told him. 'Bandits have the habit of doing that. Think yourself lucky you got most of it back.' He saw no need to be tactful with people who had openly expressed a desire to be rid of him.

Grey looked embarrassed. 'We've been thinking about a permanent sheriff.'

'You have one right under your noses,' Hewitt said. 'Charley used to help out Sheriff Anderson and he's a good man.'

'But he's a half-breed,' one council member protested. 'White men won't take orders from a half-breed.'

'They will, if he has a gun in his hand.'

'We were thinking of offering you the job,' Grey said awkwardly. 'If you're interested we can work out conditions of employment.'

Hewitt thought for a while. The job or the extra money might not be enough to hold him in Appsley but a certain young lady had to be considered.

Two hours later the town had a new sheriff and a reliable, half-breed deputy who could be hired when needed. He left the meeting and hurried across the street to the Macgregors' store. Trying not to look excited he strolled over to where Sue was standing behind the counter. 'You're looking at Appsley's new sheriff,' he announced.

Sue flashed the smile that had enchanted him since their first meeting. 'That's good news. We are very lucky to have you.

Hewitt shook his head. 'I'm the lucky one. If I hadn't found the base of that twenty-gauge shell and had a lot of luck after that, the Appsley raid would still be a big mystery.' He paused. 'That reminds me. There's one more loose end to tie up. I have some sad news for the Bramleys. There was no reward for Willie Freeman or indeed for any of the raiders.

Mullane had a minor criminal record but nothing serious.'

'Forget them,' Sue said. 'The raid is history now. You need someone to help you settle in, someone who really knows the town.'

'Are you volunteering?'

'I might as well. You need someone to keep you out of trouble.'